# My love story in broken English

*A novel*

To Madeline:
Best wishes,
Ainalem

Ainalem Tebeje

My love story in broken English



ISBN 978-1-77216-132-8

*Cover design by Vicky Amullo*

Printed by:
duProgrès Printing

Published by

Baico Publishing Inc.
E-mail: info@baico.ca
www.baico.ca

# To Canada

Lord, heed not my complaint,
Of winters that bite,
Of hard work, little respite,
Of high taxes and no returns,
Of society with prejudice,
And a nation with growing pains.

Lord, heed not my complaint, truly,
For I am grateful sincerely,
For giving me this country,
To cherish and value,
Proud to call my own.

Alas, how does one show a love so deep?
Meagre are my means, I have no gift,
I cannot write, nor can I sing,
Flawed is my English, my French so little.

To Canada, this book, I dedicate,
To say un grand merci,
For I am no more refugee.

Ainalem Tebeje

# ACKNOWLEDGEMENT

- *Praise be to St. Tekle-Haimanot for guiding me through this project during my darkest hour, grieving the death of my husband, the late Dr. Joseph Manyoni.*

- *My sincere thanks to all those who supported me in the making of this book: Baico Publishing, Vicky Amullo, Ruth Latta, Denise Amyot, Clyde Sanger.*

- *My love to the two precious jewels of the Tebeje family: Nathan Tezazu Berihun and his sister, Eldana Tezazu Berihun.*

# Chapter One

## My love story in broken English

I am Almaz Tefera.

This is my love story; this love that I carried deep inside my heart as I paddled the tumultuous river of life, travelling through continents, crossing deserts and surviving death. Its roots go back to the old, wrinkled land, which was mentioned some forty times in both the Old and New Testaments[1]; and where the Prophet Mohamed told his followers to go and seek refuge from persecution.

Ethiopia, the ancient Kingdom of the Queen of Sheba, the phoenix that keeps rising from the ashes is where my story begins. I am now in a faraway land that stretches from ocean to ocean to ocean, whose Indigenous owners kept its doors wide open and filled it with people like me. We affectionately call it Canada.

A student of English as a Second Language, I was taught by a gifted educator, we called Teacher Irene. After two years of hard work, Teacher Irene gave her class an assignment to

1 Psalms 68:31 Ethiopia shall stretch her arms unto God.

write our stories "*even if it is in broken English,*" she told us. My classmates wrote about immigration, separation, war and persecution. Mine was a love story so I have called it, "*My love story in broken English*"

Here it is, simple and plain.

It all started one morning when I woke up with a headache, one of those silly headaches that I always refused to acknowledge and treated with indifference, even contempt. In my village, no one died from headaches, so, we had no regard for illnesses that come and go. We called them the morning dew, meaning here now, gone by noon. We, the God-fearing villagers of Siqualla, dreaded only those plagues that come once and when they leave, an entire village is wiped out.

But this silly headache of mine turned out to be different. To my surprise, it moved down to my eyes, turned around my ears and threatened to invade my entire body. It felt like a loud thunder, announcing the arrival of the rains after a two-year drought. So, I named it Madam Thunder. In my village, headaches are always female and death is male.

Madam Thunder was ignored for a few days when we finally decided to seek elder advice. In my village, no patient was treated before consulting the elders. But Siqualla elders did not believe in some white-robed doctor who put stuff into your mouth and claimed to see the invisible. Worse, they knifed you with a needle to shed your precious blood which was then collected into a bottle and taken to an unknown location for some voyeur to see the disease. So, we stayed away from people who poked us, bled us and pretended to hear our inside voices.

In truth, in Siqualla, no one was ever seen by the medicine man. Those who were taken to his shop were so sick that they all died. We heard that, in a shop full of gadgets, the doctor could never bring back to life a single dead person. So we never bothered going there.

In my case, the decision was to treat me with the holy water from St. Tekle-Haimanot Church. This one-legged Ethiopian saint was touched by God Himself. As a monk, it was said that he stood on one foot, praying for such a very long time that the standing foot literally fell off from sheer exhaustion. When the foot came off, a wing sent by God appeared where it used to be. Peter Cowther wrote this poem for St. Tekle-Haimanot.

A more surprising saint there's not,
Than Abune[2] Tekle-Haimanot,
He is my all-time favourite saint,
There is none other quite so quaint.
He spent his time converting kings,
And once he sprouted several wings.

This monk, later promoted to saint, was now entrusted to cure me from Madam Thunder. To collect the holy water from his church, the elders chose a group of virtuous men who were physically fit and spiritually right. When the holy bath started, every morning, the men brought a number of huge clay pots filled with the holy water to the brim. I was then taken to a room where the women disrobed me and had me seated on a three-legged stool. Once seated, a full bucket of water was poured all over me to wash away the disease. This, of course, was a proven medicine for all those with a blind faith in the powers of St. Tekle-Haimanot.

---

2 Abune means father

I am ashamed to say this, but Madam Thunder had proven difficult for St. Tekle-Haimanot. Originally planned for three days, the period for holy bath was extended to seven, fourteen and finally twenty-one days, with little result. It was then concluded that my faith was not strong enough to fight off the silly headache. In fact, no one had accepted the fact that a simple headache was winning over this saint of miracles. One group of peasants insisted that the saint was going to act in time.

"*What is a headache, when he can actually bring back people from the brink of death,*" they said.

The second group argued that there were times when St. Tekle-Haimanot was so slow that some people did die. This, however, was said in an almost inaudible voice, so I could not swear that I heard every word. To be honest, I never heard anyone say this with authority. The truth, however, was that my headache had prevailed over the saint and I was dying a slow death.

In the end, it was concluded that what I had was not a silly headache, but a killer monster. With much regret, the elders finally conceded that some other intervention was needed to save a young bride from an imminent death. Every time I heard the words "young bride", I felt love, a love so powerful that it woke me up from dead several times. I will tell you all about my love, but first about myself.

In Siqualla, it was improper to speak highly of oneself; yet, those smart villagers had invented a subtle way of bragging, using understatements like, "*I have a roof over my head, a piece of rug to cover my back and some crumbs to nourish my stomach*", meaning this was a life of abundance. If I told you, "I can pass for a woman", it meant that my beauty was such that no man was immune from my charms.

Known as the land of music, literature and beauty, Siqualla had produced so many beautiful women that this statement was actually a fact, not bragging. Yet, my beauty was unique. Village commentators often said that while God had spent six days to create the earth and its contents, it took him a full day to making just me. The only reason I was created, they said, was to show off God's creativity. If God was the architect, I was simply the best piece of art he ever designed. In Siqualla, beauty was always defined as "Almaz Tefera."

Black as the midnight sky without stars, long as the Blue Nile and wavy like the Sahara Desert, my hair covered my entire back like a velvety shawl. My face, ebony carving of precision, harmony and tranquility, was put together by God Himself, taking care that I would be an enduring centre of attraction. Huge, almond shaped, draped by thick, long lashes, my eyes shone with a permanent ray of light. Flat with two cute openings, my nose was the epicenter people used to describe my beauty. Brownish in colour and swollen as if stung by an angry bee, my lips looked like they had a permanent smear of honey, probably a remnant of that sting.

Let me now come to God's true piece of art – my teeth. No colour white could adequately describe the whiteness of my teeth. If God had spent a full day to making me, my teeth must have taken half of that time. Every time I checked my face in a broken piece of mirror, I took time to compare my teeth against each other. Only God could line up thirty some pieces with such perfection. In my village, the comment was, "That not a single tooth stood out is a sign of total obedience to God."

My height was a perfect sum of my neck, torso, behind, thighs and legs. No portion of my body stood out as to create a miscalculation. Like the camels of the Danakil

Desert, I moved with an arresting grace, slowly, deliberately, orchestrating my movements, demanding full attention.

My physical beauty was complemented by my intellect which village commentators compared to that of the Queen of Sheba who travelled to Jerusalem to learn from King Solomon's wisdom. But this comparison was never appreciated by my father who always complained,

"*The Queen brought back an illegitimate son, not wisdom.*"

This I found unfair because, in all likelihood, the Queen of Sheba was raped by King Solomon who tricked her into entering an impossible accord which he used to sleep with the virgin queen. This is how it happened.

*Upon arrival, the Queen of Sheba was hosted to a lavish feast, attended by high priests and invited guests. Sensing his lascivious desire, the queen had warned the king on this night that he was not to touch her. So long she agreed not to take anything of his while his guest; the king accepted her request to respect her.*

*But, he tricked her by feeding her extremely spicy meal which made her thirsty in the middle of the night. Looking for water, she found the glass the king deliberately left by her side. When she tried to reach it, he surfaced out of nowhere and declared that she broke her end of the agreement. She had to pay the price.*

*The Queen swallowed her Ethiopian pride, slept with the king and returned with a royal foetus that became Prince Menelik. This illegitimate son of the Queen of Sheba and King Solomon, believed to have brought the Ark of the Covenant into Ethiopia, is perhaps responsible for the enduring bond between Ethiopians and the Israelites.*

I confess: According to village historians, Siquallans are rumoured to be the fruits of this unholy affair. This is how it happened:

*Having learnt about King Solomon, Menelik so wanted to meet his father that he travelled the same journey his mother made when he was conceived. When they met, the king knew that this indeed was his son not only because of the likeness but also because Menelik was wearing the ring that King Solomon gave to the Queen of Sheba.*

*Following their intimacy, the king was said to have presented his ring to the queen, saying, "Should you conceive from this union, this is the ring our child should wear when he comes to meet me." This ring was kept with great care until the son came of age and was presented as evidence that he was the son of King Solomon.*

*At the end of his son's visit, King Solomon suggested that Menelik settle down in Israel and assume his royal duties. Menelik instead chose to go back to his mother. Upon his departure, Solomon presented his son with a group of young Israeli men to accompany him and settle down as his subjects in the Kingdom of the Queen of Sheba. These Israeli men met Ethiopian women and settled down in the then Zagwe dynasty where Siqualla was located.*

All this to say that my roots do go back to the Queen of Sheba.

# Chapter Two

I digress: Let me now tell you who I am. The youngest of five children, I was engaged when I was in my mother's womb. This is how it happened: With four sons in the family, the news of a fifth pregnancy sent my father on a frenzy campaign of promises and prayers for a girl. One of the promises, made to a valued friend, was,

*"If the fifth child is a girl, I give her to you as a daughter-in-law."*

In response, the valued friend bowed as low as he could and said,

*"What an honour to join your family. I accept this gift of God with great responsibility. In return, I give you my word of honour that I will value her like my own child. I will give her a place of pride in my family and protect her dignity with my life.*

*"I will stand by your side when she is born, at her wedding and when she becomes a mother. And, if by God's will you depart before me, I will take your place as her true father,"* the valued friend assured my father.

What I was to become in life was determined on this very day by two men in an exchange of a vow of friendship. With this vow, my fate was sealed permanently. As it turned out, I became the fifth child, the much desired girl who gave immense pride to my father who boasted that he was, after all, capable of producing a girl.

But, mine was not a happy arrival because my mother died during delivery. This tragedy half killed my father so the valued friend had to step in as the second father to five of us.

Motherless, with no sister, I was raised by men. What I lacked as a motherless child, I gained as a child of a doting father, a sister of protective brothers and a daughter-in-law of a man who came into my life without my choice.

The first ten years of my life were half-nomadic as I was taken from home to home for training in womanhood: cooking, baking, brewing, knitting, basket weaving, cotton-spinning, hair plaiting. Coming from a long line of traditional healers, I was also taught how to identify and use plants for different ailments.

At home, a priest came regularly to teach me the Ethiopian alphabets so I could read the Bible. During my visits to my grandmothers and aunts, I was told about the secrets women use to please, fight, defeat or humiliate men. I took my lessons to heart and excelled in almost everything.

I cooked the most delicious wot[3]. I wove mind-boggling baskets, I knitted cotton shawls that surpassed the beauty of silk and brewed the most intoxicating drink. Also, I never forgot what women told me, "*Men are the enemies women raise.*"

Barely ten, I was given the responsibility of looking after the family, in charge of keeping five men fed, clean and respected. Day after day, I cooked, baked, brewed, again baked, cooked, and brewed, keeping my brothers happy and my father proud. This I did at a cost. Growing up, nobody saw me sleeping because I was always the first to get up and the last to go to bed.

---

[3] Stew in the Amharic language

Every morning, I heard the men echo a collective deafening snore while I busily prepared their breakfast. Every evening, I went to bed only after the last member of the family was securely in bed, fast asleep. My nights were full of worries about how fast the food was running out and what to cook the next day.

Every night, I stayed awake until my eyelids closed involuntarily and my body, exhausted with labour, felt half numb. I became the pride of the family not only for cooking, baking, or brewing but also for overcoming what they called a weakness, "sleep". The collective boast of the family was,

"*We never saw Almaz sleep. And yet, look at her, a work of art.*"

It never occurred to me that this was unfair; in fact, it felt good to hear them praise St. Tekle-Haimanot for giving the family a daughter.

After four years of hard labour, I turned fourteen. This was past the age when girls were prepared for marriage. Any other family would suffer a secret shame that there was a fourteen-year old virgin in the house, waiting for a proposal.

If, by fifteen, a girl was not chosen for a prospective husband, her best chance would be some thirty-year old widower, a grumpy, old father of five in search of carnal pleasure. This would remain a black mark on the family as one with a fifteen-year old spinster. Where I come from, there was no greater shame.

My family had no such problem. You will remember that I was given as a daughter-in-law to a valued friend who accepted me as a token of friendship. I was never told that I was engaged to be married to one of the valued friend's sons. Yet, by age eight, I figured out that this man who kept eyeing me with fatherly care and strange curiosity was related to me in some weird way. First, I noticed that his presence in our home brought some inexplicable discomfort on the part of my father who always checked to see if I was presentable. Then, there was a giggle here, a giggle there every time his name came up in conversation.

I added up my brothers' giggles and my father's uneasiness and arrived at a conclusion – this man was no other than my future father-in-law. Immediately, I embarked on my next secret investigation: Who among his sons would be my future husband? The valued friend had eight children, three daughters and five sons. Of the five boys, three were already committed to other families. I ruled out the fourth because he was barely two years older than me. Where I come from, we say that men take longer than women to mature, so a difference of a few years must be allowed between husband and wife.

After these calculations, I was ready to say who of the sons was going to be my future husband. And I guessed right. I must tell you more about my future husband. By age three, this boy was speaking a full language…I mean he was speaking in words, sentences, using a noun, a verb and an adjective. He could express emotions such as disappointment, frustration and hope as if he had experienced them.

When guests arrived, he welcomed them with a greeting that had the sweetness of a child and the wisdom of an adult. His mother claimed that she never had to tell him what to do or not to do. He knew right from wrong and avoided the latter like the notorious plagues of Siqualla.

News about this child travelled far beyond our village and reached the capital city of Addis Ababa where villagers were viewed as unimaginative, backward creatures who remained exactly the way God created Adam and Eve – or was it just Adam? There was this cruel joke about our village that kept city dwellers amused:

*God ordered to be taken on a tour of the globe so he could see what happened to his creatures. During his tour, he could not recognize any of the continents, oceans or mountains he created because civilization had changed them all.*

*Then, out of the blue, there was Siqualla, tucked behind big cities, devoid of signposts, landmarks, roads or tracks. Surprised that there was this village that remained unchanged, God said, "I remember this place. It is exactly how I created it."*

This unkind joke was told to show that we never caught up with civilization.

Going back to our gifted boy, a wealthy Samaritan who heard about his story offered to raise him as a city boy. At age five, the little boy was separated from his family and taken to Addis Ababa for schooling. This man, also called "*Uncle*", had supposedly told villagers that the boy needed modern schooling and not the traditional rural education of Siqualla.

Indeed, the urban-style schooling offered in cities was quite different from what we called education in Siqualla. With its structured system of pupils, teachers, administrators, rules and regulations, the objective of schooling was modernization. In Siqualla, the sole purpose of education was to read the Bible and become good Christians.

The first stage of education, which was to read and write, required mastering the 182 Ethiopian syllables (26 characters each with seven forms). The second stage was to master the First Epistle General of St. John in the ancient language of

Geez[4]. In the third stage, a student would study the Acts of the Apostles, followed by the fourth stage which consisted of the Psalms of David, the Praises to God, the Virgin Mary and the Songs of Solomon and of the Prophets.

As time passed, the story of this five-year old who had left his birthplace for schooling grew into a myth throughout the village. He was the first and only living thing to have left our village for city life. Growing up, we all heard about this boy who was taken to the city and when we asked what happened to him, we were told that he was being schooled.

Indeed he proved to be a scholar. By age ten, he had completed eight years of elementary school. At fourteen, he graduated from secondary school and four years later he received a degree with distinction. On his graduation, he received an award of substantial funding for an education project in our village.

Two years later, aged twenty, he arrived back in Siqualla, armed with a certificate, a high school diploma and a degree in pedagogy. Upon his arrival in our village, he was overheard declaring his intentions:

"*I am here to open a school, teach every boy and girl and bring civilization to Siqualla.*"

As we say in Siqualla, "*Legless, yet rumour travels the fastest.*" In no time, news about a plan for schooling spread throughout the village, igniting the first rural revolution in Siqualla. The next day, the entire village came out to protest against the boy. Led by priests, their hands stretched to the sky, elders beseeched God to spare them from what they

[4] Geez is an ancient Semitic language, still used as the liturgical language in Ethiopian Orthodox churches.

called the urban curse, conniving to attract boys and girls to the city.

Every single villager had a complaint. Fathers said that boys were to be taken away from the much valued work of shepherding. Mothers complained that, without daughters, they would not be able to take care of the children, look after the elderly and feed the men and boys. Children joined their parents, grumbling that they were to be taken to the city where people did not grow their own food.

This was the home-coming our young man received from Siqualla. When the gathering arrived in front of his parents' house, the city boy was asked to step out and tell them what he was up to. In response, he delivered a speech that changed Siqualla's fate.

*"Honoured elders, respected parents, beloved brothers and sisters:*

*"My name is Lemma Tessema. I was born and raised here till age five when I was taken by Uncle to get urban schooling in Addis Ababa. I am now twenty years old. For fifteen years, I dreamt of Siqualla – of our churches, the ravines, the mountains and the fields.*

*"In my dreams, I saw your faces and heard your voices. I heard the laughter of the shepherds as they came back home with their cattle and saw the women, with pots on their backs, going to the river.*

*"Every time I woke up from these dreams, I wept. The longer I was separated from Siqualla, the stronger became my sense of belonging. So, I decided to hurry up, finish my schooling and rush back to Siqualla. And, here I am.*

*"Siqualla is my home and you are my people. Yet, barely five-year old, I was taken away because we did not have a*

*single school here. We still are without one. If we do not open a school, more children will be taken away for city life and urban schooling. Some will follow my example and come back; others will never see Siqualla again. So, if you want your children to stay around, we must open a school here.*

*"You might ask, what will a school do in Siqualla when we have our own priests to teach us the Bible? I assure you this school will offer Bible classes where one priest can teach several pupils at the same time.*

*"Every time you sell your produce to city merchants, you depend entirely on the traders who always take advantage of our ignorance. When we complain, we are constantly told to do the calculations ourselves, knowing well that we cannot. This school will put an end to this exploitation because I will teach your children how to add, subtract, divide and multiply.*

*"In Siqualla, childbirth has become a death sentence for young women because they have only half a chance to survive. If I open this school, midwives will be trained in better methods. There will no longer be funerals for new mothers and the fear of growing up motherless will be history.*

*"Yes, farming is our life and our life is about farming. Siqualla farmers are renowned for their ability to read the clouds. By looking up to the skies, a farmer can tell whether the rains will come early, late or on time. He can predict the amount of the rains and the frequency of the rainfall. These forecasts about drought and floods rarely fail. But, when they do, we have no other recourse but to go hungry because we do not use this ancient knowledge to prepare for the lean days. This school will teach you all you need to know about growing food that will feed your family, not from hand to mouth, but from year to year.*

*"I am asking for your blessing to run the school for one year. Your children will tell you what they learned every day. If you do not like it, we will close down the school and I will go back to the capital city and I promise to you that I will not come back."*

A twenty-year old boy had finally managed to disturb the long slumber of our village. As he spoke, the silence was intermittently disturbed by sobs, the sniffling of the noses and the sucking sound Siquallans make when they are awed. The speech had something to offer to every child, parent and elder in Siqualla.

The promise to change childbirth from a time of grief to a time of celebration was too attractive to ignore. Equally attractive was the promise to end the trade exploitation. Of course, the end of our hand-to-mouth existence was too good to believe, but, at the same time, too good to pass up.

Village commentators later said that the address had the markings of both urban subtleties and rural openness. It certainly had the finesse of schooling – confidence and strategy. Yet, it was full of rural attributes – honesty and respect. By choosing powerful words, the young man had unleashed fear and instilled hope, both at the same time. Masked with what looked like a compliment, the speech had a certain element of criticism. Although the delivery had the tone of pleading, they could not miss the warning within it. All in all, it was agreed that this was a message crafted to change Siqualla forever.

The next day, a miracle happened. Not only was Siqualla awake, but also in a hurry to accept change. Every man, woman and child who had protested the previous day came back, this time singing a different tune. They came out in unison, guided by one desire and held together by a common objective: to build a school. Every human, animal and man-made thing carried something: stone, wood, soil, water, grass, cord…anything to build a school. In their hearts, the men and women brought hope, determination and a small burden of apprehension.

A week later, the St. Tekle-Haimanot School was officially opened at a ceremony attended by priests, village elders and prospective students. The next day, pupils turned out in dozens, too many for a one-room school, so the young teacher decided to run morning, afternoon and evening shifts. Of the entire village, not a single girl was registered. When parents were asked why, the response was, "*Girls are too important in the house to be spared for education.*"

On the opening day, each student received a package of books, note books, and a set of pencils, erasers and pencil sharpeners. The classroom was furnished with benches, desks, a blackboard and chairs, all used, some broken, apparently donated by supporters of schooling and secretly imported to Siqualla.

The first few weeks of school brought total chaos with hilarious and sad anecdotes told about students and their parents. On the first day of school, parents came with their children and remained in the classroom, saying that they wanted to see things for themselves. A full week was wasted due to this problem. Then, there were others. The funny anecdotes had to do with those bored students who simply walked out of classroom to play hide and seek, while the teacher, still inside, was busy giving lesson. In other cases, a father would simply barge into the classroom and ask,

"Son, *where did you put the axe? I have been looking for it all day.*"

The sad stories were about students who were permanently taken out of school because they were unable to tell their parents how to double their farm yield one day after the first class.

Thanks to the way the teacher introduced the new system, slowly a sense of order prevailed. First, he started by explaining that shepherding was different from schooling and the transition from one to the other needed some unlearning. For example, the shepherd's time which was measured by sunrise and sunset was now replaced by classroom time of hours and minutes.

Then, there was a lesson about academic discipline, being different from the discipline of shepherding. In shepherding, mobility was mandatory as opposed to the stillness demanded in classrooms. Shepherds could afford to wander in their thoughts while education required full attention. In shepherding, it was all about sharing. In education, you received what the teacher gave.

Shepherding was about negotiation, give and take between the shepherd who kept his herd within his confines and his cattle constantly seeking to venture into other spaces. Education was quite the opposite.

Next was a lesson about schooling being similar to shepherding, but this time, the teacher was the shepherd and his students the cattle. A good shepherd took his cattle to fertile pasture where the grass was green and the water plenty. A good teacher imparted knowledge that made his students think, solve problems and strive to become better.

A good shepherd, like Christ, would go to look for his lost sheep. A good teacher would take time to help that weak student. A shepherd who slumbered on duty was likely to let his cattle wander into the wrong field. A careless teacher would certainly miss the signs of a class that had lost interest in learning.

Within months, Siqualla was thoroughly infatuated with schooling. We were all talking about schooling as,

*"The road that leads from darkness to light, from ignorance to knowledge, from poverty to affluence, from despair to hope, from cruelty to kindness, from disease to health and from oppression to freedom."*

Anyone with urban schooling was called "*smart, generous, very important and good looking.*" A new word, "*unschooled*" was coined as the most demeaning insult. Yet, if schooling had added anything to our life, we were yet to see it.

After some time, elders started complaining about signs of urban influence. This observation came about when pupils started explaining to their parents that diseases were caused by germs and bacteria and could be cured only by dealing with the cause. This was a direct affront to the villagers who believed that diseases were caused and cured by God and only God.

Finally, the followers of the "education camp" had had it. They declared their decision to stand up to the "school camp", so the claim that schooling was the road from cruelty to kindness or from hatred to love was systematically challenged, and defeated. The attributes that were coined to praise schooled people as kind, generous and good-looking were discredited one by one. That schooling was a panacea for every rural ailment was ridiculed to no end.

By the end of the academic year, half of the students had dropped out. Yet, with fifty percent graduation, the teacher could not be happier. On graduation day, he hosted a huge feast to mark the historic occasion. He slaughtered a fat cow and the women and girls, who else, were asked to cook the food.

Someone called a Government man came to hand out pieces of paper which, we were told, were called "certificates" and were the only proof that a schooled person was indeed schooled. To conclude the ceremony, the Government man was asked to address the gathering. Back in their neighbourhood, the villagers gathered for the customary post-mortem. On the speech by Government man, they all confessed that they did not understand what he was saying.

"*True, he did speak our language, but it did not speak to us,*" they agreed.

This was followed by a lively discussion as to what, after all, was government. Different people used different pronouns to refer government as a "he, she or it". Truth be told, since its creation by the compassionate Lord, Siqualla never had a government. Nor was there a need for one. For example, Siqualla never had courts, prisons, judges or lawyers to administer justice. No doctors, nurses or hospitals to provide health care. We never had politicians, public servants or bureaucracy to tax us. In Siqualla, we had God and, next to Him, each other.

Certainly, we did not function in a vacuum. We had a system to raise children and honour elders, to shame the guilty and penalize the criminal, to heal the sick, bury the dead and console the bereaved. So, we failed to see what else the government would be doing that Siqualla villagers were not already doing. At the end of the debate, there was only a huge laughter…all at the expense of government.

# Chapter Three

Two months after the graduation, while Siqualla was busy farming and harvesting, we were taken by a huge surprise: an invasion by city dwellers sent by the government to build a school in our village. Within weeks, the crew built a bigger school with several rooms, put up a fence around the school, dug a well for drinking water, erected private out-houses for girls and boys and planted trees for students to enjoy some shade during lunch break.

When we found out that two more teachers were being brought from the capital city and that they would be staying in Siqualla during the academic year, we felt as if aliens were about to invade us. Of all that had happened, the news about teachers residing amongst us had our priests weep openly. They grieved for rural education which, they said, was on its death bed.

Now, Siqualla had a school for over 100 students. There would be grades one and two. As for girls, the government made it mandatory that one daughter per family attend school. Worried parents were assured that there would be separate classrooms for girls and boys. When the elders asked why they were not consulted about this ahead of time, they were warned, "*Are you trying to defy the government*?"

Our elders who knew when to fight back and when to retreat decided to surrender. They all knew that, this time, there was no pleading by Lemma Tessema, the young scholar with a dream to bring civilization to Siqualla. This time, it was the government with its harsh announcements, stern warnings and something called "deadlines".

As it turned out, this was only the beginning of Siqualla's transition from the way God created it to the way government would be creating it. As we were to find out, the government continued its invasion, introducing health and justice systems, along with a tax system. Lemma Tessema was apparently behind all this. If the elders regretted his return, it was now too late to do anything about it. In his quiet unassuming way, my future husband was determined to change Siqualla single handed, one system at a time.

While Siqualla was going through this historic transition, something big was happening in our family. One morning in September, just before school opened, a delegation of five men arrived in our house "unexpectedly". This was the day when we all performed the traditional charade.

The first pretence was successfully carried out by the men who said that they had come to visit my father, whom they had not seen for a long time. This fake pronouncement was followed by an equally artificial response by my father, who not only feigned a huge surprise to see the delegates but also pleaded,

*"In the name of St. Tekle-Haimanot, I urge you to come in and take a short rest."*

Charade aside, this was the delegation sent by my father-in-law to present the official proposal for marriage. As soon as they walked in, the elders announced their decision not to touch a morsel of bread before they presented the true purpose of their visit.

When allowed to proceed, they started with a lengthy lecture about the importance of marriage, the friendship of the two families to be united and the need for girls to settle down early. They added,

*"Remember, your daughter was not born when you gave your word of honour to your friend, Tessema."*

*"Having lost her mother, Almaz is all I have in this world,"* said my father in his heart-wrenching response, *"She is my consolation prize from St. Tekle-Haimanot. I need to be assured that she will be joining a family that will love and respect her. As for this "schooled man", I pray to St. Tekle-Haimanot that he will be like a brother, a friend and a husband who provides well."*

Proposal accepted, the delegates settled down to enjoy a feast of delicious food and special drink, prepared ahead of time in expectation of the visit. The wedding date was set for after Easter at the end of the long and harsh Lent when the killing of animals, eating meat, drinking milk and enjoying the pleasures of life, including sex, music and drinking were prohibited.

Aged fourteen, I was now ready to marry a man I had never met, barely saw and hardly loved. Very soon, I would be facing my wedding day, the riskiest and scariest period of my life. According to married women, wedding nights were filled with frightening stories of what we called the *encounter*, a word invented to camouflage the intimacy between a man and a woman.

On this night, I would be forced to engage in the *encounter* so as to be tested for virginity, a sign of family honour and social respectability. This *encounter* starts with an excruciating pain caused by the penis forcefully penetrating through the frigid vagina of a virgin. This is then followed by gushing blood, sometimes mixed with urine, as the virginity membrane is torn by sheer force and a fresh opening is made for the penis to continue its invasion. Then, the eternity of what feels like sand paper going in and out until the heavy weight of a fulfilled beast rests on the bride's chest, creating a huge sense of fear.

To add to all this, what if schooling had turned this man into a monster and instead of losing my virginity I lost my life on my wedding night? After all, in our village, city dwellers were viewed as selfish creatures, blinded by worldly pleasures. Sheer terror overwhelmed me, followed by poor appetite, insomnia and loss of weight.

In preparation of the wedding day, our house was turned into a community laboratory where women camped, from September to April, to prepare, from scratch, everything necessary for the big day. Both my grandmothers came to stay with us for the whole eight months, a great delight for me, as some of my responsibilities were transferred to them.

Every day, women turned up with ideas, advice, free labour and gossip. Some volunteered a few hours a day, others a day or two a week and still others a few nights every now and then. All this was on top of their family and community duties, including, cooking, baking, brewing, fetching water, collecting wood, cleaning churches, washing clergy outfits, visiting the sick and consoling the bereaved.

Most of the time, these women reminisced about their wedding nights, how they had faked headache or nausea, and put up a desperate fight to push the *encounter* by just one night. In all the marriages of Siqualla, not a single bride had ever succeeded in postponing the *encounter*. According to our culture, husbands must perform the *encounter* because society demands that the bride must be tested for virginity on her wedding night.

The women did reveal though that the only exception was when husbands failed to perform because their thing refused to stand up. What? I did hear about "the thing" but never knew that the thing stands up or sits down. But, who does one ask? Any sign of curiosity would put me on the list of "loose women in a hurry to enjoy carnal pleasure." I convinced myself to look disinterested, but kept praying that Lemma Tessema's thing would decide to sit down permanently.

Every time my father saw the women busy in our house, he beamed with joy and complimented them. On this particular day, he said,

"*Only in Siqualla can one find such generosity. Who says my Almaz is motherless when she has all of you? St. Tekle-Haimanot is rewarding me for the grief I suffered in losing her mother.*

"*I cannot possibly return your kindness, but this I can do: I promise to give Almaz's first daughter to one among your sons. We will decide later whose son, in the meantime, this is my word of honour and you can count on it.*"

Given that the promise was made to women, it was first received as tentative. Soon after, my father was approached by a man for a serious conversation about this promise. Once more, my father who shaped my destiny some fourteen years ago was about to decide the fate of my daughter who was yet to be conceived.

A couple of months before the wedding, I was told that I would be confined to the house to protect me from potential risks due to the merciless sun, angry wind, biting cold, freak accidents and silly infections that could easily disrupt wedding plans. During these two months, the women worked on me to prepare me for a happy marriage.

The first lesson was about survival skills: communication, negotiation, mental prowess. Next, it was a lesson about managing mother-in-law's interference and son-influence.

Then, the women moved on to working on my physical beauty. First, the hair was treated with fresh butter, known for its nourishing effects. By milking the cows, the women churned the milk to produce chunks of butter. Once my hair was plaited into five-six rows, the women had access to the skull to smear the skin with layers of butter. After a couple of days, the hair was washed, plaited and buttered again. This was repeated four-five times until the hair was brought back to its natural beauty.

Then, it was my body's turn. From a nearby bush, the women collected leaves, roots, bark pieces, petals, and seeds, known for their healing properties. These were ground into powder and added to fresh honey, making a thick aromatic paste which was smeared all over my arms and legs, while the women gave me a gentle massage to exfoliate the dead cells, revealing smooth baby skin. After numerous sessions of this treatment, I was cured from the fatigue I had accumulated since age ten.

A few weeks before the wedding, the focus shifted to my face which I stopped washing with water. Instead, it was rubbed with lemon, rinsed with fresh milk, and smeared with fresh butter. Every morning, I was given slender pieces of wood, cut from a local tree, known for ingredients that removed stain, refreshed breath and whitened teeth.

Finally, I was made to drink a mixture of plants to detox my internal organs. This drink gave me a runny stomach until I voided pure liquid, clean like fresh water, with no colour or smell. At the same time, I was given the customary bride's etiquette lessons,

*"Never chatter,*

*"Keep the head low, avoid direct eye gaze,*

*"Eat small portions, chew with your mouth closed, and swallow real slow,*

*"Do not gulp, sip water,*

*"Avoid food that produces gas."*

It was during this counsel that I was reminded of an ancient story:

*Soon after her marriage, this bride was weaving a basket, sitting next to her in-laws. When she pulled the grass she was using to make a basket, the contact between her sweaty fingers and the grass produced a sound that sounded like farting. The in-laws recognized this as the normal sound often heard during basketry, so they paid no attention, unaware that the bride lacked this knowledge.*

*Unfortunately, the bride was convinced that the in-laws had suspected her of farting. So, she quietly left the room and hanged herself to save the honour of her family from the social shame associated with a farting bride.*

But, I digress. My wedding was now a few days away. Relatives started arriving from near and far with wedding gifts. My favourite uncle brought a cow, other relatives presented sheep, chickens and bushels of grain. My grandmother gave me her only jewellery, an old, tarnished silver cross, with black thread in the loop, serving as a chain. My other grandmother, on my mother's side, presented a parcel that contained a white, hand-made embroidered cotton dress with a matching shawl. Included in this parcel was my late mother's wedding dress that was kept as my inheritance. When all was calculated, the value of the gifts received by my family far exceeded what was spent for my wedding.

From here on, the priority was to receive guests, including many who needed to be looked after as they arrived exhausted, following hours or days of journey on foot or by horse. With the arrival of relatives and friends, pure joy filled our home. There was so much love and affection; hugging and kissing; laughter and tears. Of course, there was song and dance.

My father's euphoria had no bounds as he kept saying,

"*Praise be to St. Tekle-Haimanot!! Aren't we lucky this is Siqualla? God is kind. He gave us so much and asked for nothing in return. Can you imagine if we had to buy this happiness from the market?*

"*What if we had to pay God a salary? Or, if He asked for a bribe? Happiness would be the exclusive commodity for the rich and mighty.*"

"*Hallelujah!*" they all agreed.

My wedding was now two days away. On Saturday, a hair dresser, renowned for her dexterity, was brought home to plait my hair. With her dainty fingers, using a sharp divider, she first split the loose hair into different rows. Taking a few strands at a time, she then plaited big, medium and slim rows. This took half a day, but when all was done, women commentators agreed that no words could describe something as intricate and dazzling as this hair style.

Later that day, something unusual happened. A messenger arrived unexpectedly to announce that a delegation representing the groom was on its way for a short visit. What? A groom was sending a delegation on the eve of the wedding? How dare he? Did he not know that in-laws were not allowed to set foot in the bride's home before the wedding? Or, was this another affront by "Mr. Schooled Man with his urban values?"

In no time, a crowd gathered and the wedding mood quickly turned war-like as if the enemy was on its way for a surprise attack. Men and women got busy, guessing what could be the reason for such an unexpected visit. The only motive that made sense was that they were coming to spy on our preparations so they could improve on theirs. Alas, we could not have been more wrong!!

In the midst of this pandemonium, the delegation, a woman and a man, arrived, carrying something that they said was from the groom to the bride. This too was a first for Siqualla, but it was too late to say no. The delegates asked for permission to present the contents of a suitcase. Now that I was confined to a private room, my aunts were asked to represent me in accepting the items that turned out to be gifts.

As each gift was presented, I could hear ululation, blessings and complimentary words and wondered how quickly the mood had turned from one of war into one of celebration. Mission accomplished, the delegates left, thanking the family profusely for receiving them on the eve of the wedding. Soon after, the gifts were brought to me: a pair of gold earrings, a wedding ring, a pair of shoes, a traditional wedding dress with a matching shawl, a bottle of perfume and kohl from the big city.

As I accepted each gift, I felt joy, love, pride and shyness, all stirred into one huge mixture. When I tried to hide this mixture, a big lump formed in my throat, my eyes filled with a huge flood and I burst into tears, hiding my face with two hands. They all knew that this was the beginning of the heart going tender, so one of my aunts came to my rescue, offering a much needed excuse,

"*We all know that you are crying for your mother, but remember, we are all your mothers. Aren't we?*"

The jubilation quickly left and grief entered the room as women started weeping, wiping their faces with their shawls, saying, "*Oh, if only her mother was here.*"

Only a few hours away, Sunday was the day to face my fate. To help me sleep, I was given a warm bath and milk. Whatever sleep I could manage was disturbed by a nightmare in which my husband came at me like a menacing beast. I tossed around all night, enjoying the drum beat, clapping, ululation and melodious wedding songs, coming from the huge tent. How I wanted to be part of this night! But I was to remain in a private room.

In the morning, before sunrise, a group of young women came into my room to prepare me for the wedding party which was to arrive shortly to take me to church. To help loosen raw nerves, the women kept teasing me,

"*Tomorrow this time, having given your virginity, you will be joining our rank and file*", then a roaring laughter, as they continued,

"*If you scream loud enough, we should be able to tell the time of the invasion,*" they continued laughing. I was not amused at all.

Amidst laughter and jokes, I was given a warm bath, rubbed with scented oil, dressed in my wedding outfit, bejewelled and prettified, until the women could not believe their eyes. Still playful, they warned that my beauty was such that it could easily paralyze my husband, resulting in poor *performance*. They laughed until they hurt; I remained frozen with fear.

Finally, I left the private room where I had been kept for what felt like a life-time. By keeping me isolated, the plan was first to create curiosity, then a surprise about my looks. And it worked. As I came out, I was met by a large group of family members and friends who gasped in disbelief to see my transition into what they called "an angel, a beauty, a princess, stunning, dazzling, dignified, unknown to the human eye, etc." Feeling somewhat flattered, I smiled timidly in appreciation.

On my way out, I approached my father, knelt down and kissed his right knee to ask for his blessings. In response, he gently held my shoulders with both hands, murmuring a quiet blessing. When I stood up, I saw two lines of giant tears running down his cheeks. Seeing my father weep broke my heart into pieces and I hugged him with all my love, burying my face in his chest. Someone had to tear me apart. Still weeping, my father then said,

"*My daughter, you were a mere child when you were given the responsibility of looking after this family, and you gave me immense pride in your service. Today, as you accept yet another responsibility to serve your in-laws, I would like to tell you that every morning and night, as you laboured to feed this family, I was awake, sometimes weeping, wondering how much you had to endure simply because you were a girl. Today, I stand before you to show my gratitude and respect.*"

Wiping his tears, he then announced my wedding gift: half of his entire livestock. He simply kissed me on the forehead when I protested, "*But, Father, you have barely enough for yourself.*"

Next, I asked for the blessings of my grandmothers, uncles and aunts. Finally, I headed toward my brothers who were standing together, looking lost between the happiness of the moment and the fear of a future without me. As four of them rushed towards me, we burst into one huge weeping, all four planting kisses on my cheeks, shoulders and hands. The oldest then asked for permission to announce something,

"*When you go to your in-laws, you will find a new cottage which we just built as a wedding gift from your brothers. This will be your own place where you will raise your children. Knowing your sense of privacy, we also added a private out-house, only for your use.*"

I was about to start choking with that mixture of love, happiness and pride when my aunts pulled me back to the private room to clean me up.

"*Look what you have done!*" they scolded. "*Your face is a total mess with tears and kohl all over. We have to redo the make-up.*"

Finally, it was time to join the groom's party which was patiently waiting outside. Having heard about the Siqualla beauty, Lemma Tessema was certainly dying to see me for the first time. But, no, not so quickly! Strategically positioned in the middle of a three-tiered entourage, we deliberately made sure that I was almost impossible to spot.

Right next to me was a circle of dazzling girls, dressed to the moon and sporting different hair braids, looking like brides in their own right. In the second tier was a group of mothers, young and old, dignified and proud. The third, led by my father and four brothers, was a formidable group of men.

As we approached the groom's party, the two men who had formed my destiny before I arrived in this world moved forward, walking briskly toward each other. First, they shook hands vigorously, beaming with pride over their joint accomplishment. Next, they rested their hands on each other's shoulders, a sign of mutual respect for keeping their word of honour. Then, they hugged affectionately to show that the two families were "*united to labour and harvest; to grieve and rejoice from this day onward.*"

It was then time for the coming together of the two families. Upon the instruction of my father, my entire group moved forward to greet the groom's, leaving me alone, mercilessly exposed to the groom and his party. From the slight glimpse I could manage, the same thing was happening at the other end, with the groom standing alone, as his party moved forward to meet mine.

Fourteen years after we had been committed to each other, I was about to see the groom for the first time. But, with my head bowed, I could only feel a towering figure standing next to me, uttering a few hushed words of greeting. It felt strange to be so close to him after all these years, but I had to avoid direct gaze as this would put me on the list of curious women, viewed as undesirable by society.

After a short walk, we came across admirers who told us that the entire Siqualla population was in and around the church, eagerly awaiting the arrival of the wedding party to witness the marriage of a schooled man and a peasant girl. As we got closer, we were met by a sea of humanity, so large that it was beyond my capacity to grasp.

Involuntarily, I uttered a single word of surprise, a word so faint that only the groom, being next to me, could hear. Hearing this word, he took half a step closer to me and touched my hand with what felt like one finger. This was our very first touch. Gentle and stealthy, this touch did something to my heart. It left me torn between two strange feelings: one the feeling of wanting more of it and the other, wanting none of it. I wanted to ask my aunts about this strange feeling, but now that I was surrounded by the groom's party, I had no one to share this top secret.

When we entered the church premises, we were welcomed by priests and deacons, nuns and monks, men and women, bright like the Siqualla moon, wearing their Sunday best. Inside the church, there was no room left even for air. For hours, I stood still, my head bowing down, while the clergy completed the three-hour liturgy of the Ethiopian Orthodox Church, the holy communion, the readings of the scripture and the concluding cerebration, featuring special chants composed by the 6$^{th}$ Century St. Yared of Ethiopia.

At the end of the service, we were asked to kneel down so the head priest could pronounce his blessings for a happy life filled with healthy children. Having taken Christ's body and blood, we were now united as husband and wife, only death would do us part. In the event of a most unlikely divorce, he could remarry and I would immigrate to another village where I would remain a pariah, unfit for a community life.

Flanked by adoring admirers, we slowly made our way back to my parents' where Lemma Tessema was given a historic reception. On arrival, we were received by a rowdy crowd, singing, dancing and ululating. As per tradition, the welcome songs singled out the best men for unkind words, calling them "slow, lazy and unfit for such a noble task." In response, Lemma Tessema's friends demonstrated their worth by singing loud, jumping high and taking the unkind words in good humour.

Amidst laughter, joy and excitement, we made our grand entry into the tent which was already filled with the entire village, invited by word of mouth, one peasant to another, one family to the next.

As we were led to our seats, I was filled with pride and guilt to see how much had gone into this feast. I noticed that the earth had gotten softer with the fresh, green, cut grass, generously laid all over the ground. The air was filled with the welcoming scent of the eucalyptus tree. The scruffy peasants and fatigued women were transformed into eye-pleasing beings with their bodies washed, oiled and dressed in new or almost new attires. Thanks to Siqualla women, my wedding was unprecedented in the quality and quantity of food and drink served.

And, there was my father with his usual excitement until I wished he would stop,

*"Thank God, this is Siqualla!! The good Lord who keeps giving! He who never runs out of kindness! The kind Lord who never holds back even when we hurt him! Our Lord who is quick to forgive and never holds grudges.*

*"The compassionate Lord never tires to respond to our plea! Imagine if he stopped giving every time we sinned. What if He were a government? He would tax us for the air we breathe, for our sight, for our mobility."*

After hours of entertainment, the best man said a few words of thank you, calling the marriage the first of its kind in beauty, love, and hospitality. He then uttered the dreadful words, "*We request permission to take the bride.*" In Siqualla, this part of the wedding could be compared to the mourning of a dead person. As my husband and I moved from elder to elder, asking for blessings, there was a collective expression of grief. Yes, it was time to depart.

Suddenly, it hit me. This was the time to grieve for me. A mere child, I was now to leave everyone and everything I had known since childhood to live with strangers, including the notorious mother-in-law. And to prove that there was no coming back, I was reminded of an old story:

*This young woman was so unhappy in her marriage that she decided to go back to her parents, seeking support and love. She walked a full day, travelling from her in-laws' to her parents' village, filled with a vision of a happy reception. Her ears echoed the welcoming words of her mother, the assurance of her father and the comforting laughter of siblings.*

*Just before sunset, she reached where she could see her home and what looked like her father, busily tending to the garden. So, she hastened her steps, eager to tell her story of abuse in the hands of husband and in-laws. Suddenly, the father looked up and seemed to have recognized her. Sensing that this was not a normal visit,* he asked,

*"Is this my daughter? And what brings you here?"*

*"I can't take it anymore, Father. I just can't. I am back home,"* she answered.

To make sure that she heard him, he cleared his throat, raised his voice and said,

*"This is not your home, daughter. You no longer belong to this family. Go back to your husband. That is your home now."*

*Then and there, she turned back and was never seen or heard from again.*

We all pretended that this was a true story, but the fact was that it was invented and told at critical times in order to discourage women from thinking that they could always go back home if the marriage failed.

# Chapter Four

Back to my wedding: To bid us farewell, the entire party stood in silence while the priest prayed for "*love from husband and respect from wife.*" In the end, the groom was told, "*Here is your bride to love, to support and to protect.*" But, alas, my legs froze when I was asked to get up, so I asked for my father. But he was prevented from getting close to me.

"*The usual excuse to delay departure,*" I heard someone say.

Then, to every body's shock, my husband asked, "*Can someone give her a sip of water, please?*" With this request, Lemma Tessema had just committed a cultural crime. A few rolled their eyes, some shook their heads and others made faces to show disapproval of his intervention. But he stood firm, again asking for water. His request was ignored, but as we say in Siqualla, this was when the first seed of love was planted in my heart.

After a dramatic farewell scene, I started the long journey to start a new life with a new family, so I made no effort to hide my fear or grief. I wept all the way, giving my husband a heavy heart, as he kept asking,

"*Can someone give her a sip of water, please?*"

Finally, words were not enough and, with great courage, he reached for my hands which he was shocked to find dripping with sweat. He cleaned them dry with his. For over a decade, I only heard about Lemma Tessema as the "so-called schooled man with urban values." This was our first contact where our hands joined and our sweat mixed. I was ashamed of myself that I had quietly accepted the gesture and promised that, should this happen again; I would try to control myself. In spite of my efforts to resist, with kind words and gentle touches, my husband kept planting love seeds in my heart, a single grain at a time.

Arrival at the in-laws' was equally dramatic with a long welcoming line of well-wishers, ranging from grandparents to baby nieces and nephews. Next to the family circle was another group of priests and deacons, village elders, and some urban looking people, including the two new teachers.

As we were taken around the tent, there were signs of affection, admiration and awe. Yet, the only effect this had on me was a cruel reminder that I was all alone with no one from my side.

Inside the tent, it did not take me long to see the evidence of affluence. The tent was filled with lanterns, in contrast to the shabby, hand-made candles prepared by my family. A tape-recorder was blaring the wedding songs, instead of the singers who serenaded the wedding party at my parents'. Grassless, the ground was covered with plastic flooring and draped with rugs. The benches were soft with cushions that gave me a sensational feeling when I sat down. The guests looked healthy, their clothes shiny and their demeanour assured. This indeed was a wedding of the school camp.

We were treated to an extravagant dinner financed by the rich uncle who went out of his way to give the reception an urban look and feel. Throughout the evening, guests enjoyed themselves, eating, drinking, singing and dancing. While this went on, my brain was busy, designing a strategy to survive the night.

As the evening slowly phased into night, my father-in-law addressed the party, speaking highly of my father, complimenting me for my beauty, culinary skills, healing power and mental prowess.

He ended by vowing in the name of St. Tekle-Haimanot to protect me from ill-treatment and disrespect. He then announced our wedding gift, "A *plot of land to grow food for your children.*" Choking with tears, my husband knelt down to kiss his father's knees to express his gratitude. I followed suit.

Soon after, a prominent member of the family announced that it was time "*to take the bride to her new home.*"

I must now digress to a different story: In our very long history, there had not been a single incident where a bride was found not to be a virgin in Siqualla. Yet, every single bride had gone through the virginity test. This is how it was done:

*A piece of white cloth – cotton, fresh, never used – is left inside the private room where the groom and bride retire for the night. Here, the encounter takes place; the bride loses her virginity and starts to bleed, often for the first time, since most were of pre-menstrual age. This piece of cloth is then stained with the bride's blood and presented to a group of mother elders, camped outside, waiting for the evidence of her virginity. Upon receiving the blood-stained cloth, the group declares a favourable verdict of virginity by erupting into euphoric jubilation.*

Back to my story: When the time to retire arrived, I was paralyzed from head to toe by fear that I was going to be with a man in a private room for the first time in my life. My heart leapt out of my chest when I realized that this man was actually going to harm me. All the tips and lessons from the Siqualla mothers evaporated, leaving me defenseless. I felt like a lamb entering the lion's den. To my surprise, my eyes turned into two pebbles, not a drop of tears to soften his heart.

Indeed, numb and in disbelief, I found myself alone with Lemma Tessema in a private room. Suddenly, it struck me how much I had gone through as a motherless baby, a nomadic child, a hard-working daughter and now a bride of a man I hardly knew, who was about to harm me. Sensing my fear, Lemma Tessema addressed me for the first time.

"*Are you afraid, Almaz*?" he asked.

It took this simple question to unleash a mountain of deep-seated emotions. On this night, I shed more tears than I ever had in my entire life. I never knew that it was possible for someone to cry so hard. But, I did. Taken aback, Lemma Tessema held my hands and said,

"I promise i*n the name of St. Tekle-Haimanot that I will not harm you. I am so afraid myself, we will not do anything. Please believe me. I will not touch you tonight.*"

I hardly believed him. How about the virginity test? Wasn't he required to present the blood-stained evidence to the mother elders as a proof of my virginity? Siqualla women had told me that this evidence was so crucial that it could never be delayed, postponed or cancelled under any circumstances. No bride would be recognized as faithful in the absence of such evidence. This evidence had such a value that it could make or break a bride. So, I concluded that Lemma Tessema was only playing a game to calm me down before proceeding with his invasion.

But, no, my fear was unfounded because the groom had indeed a plot to get us out of this predicament. He told me that he was going to cut himself, stain the piece of cloth with his own blood and submit it as proof of my virginity. He said that since this was never done, no one would suspect that we had produced false evidence.

Almost whispering, he warned me that this was a very serious offence and, if found out, there would be a great shame to us, to our families and we would be ostracized as if we had committed a crime or a sin. As he said this, I could see that he was filled with fear and guilt that we were about to be the first couple to violate Siqualla's most cherished value. Urging me to treat the ploy as our wedding vow, he said,

"*I feel conflicted to do this, but no price is high enough for our love. We must now swear to die with this secret.*"

Sitting on a stool, he then took out a fresh razor, made an incision on his leg and asked me to hand him the piece of cloth which was soaked in no time as he kept bleeding, forming a small red puddle right under his feet. When I saw his desperate attempt to put the situation under control, I went down on my knees, covered his wound with my wedding shawl, the one he had given me, and kept my finger pressed on the right spot.

Still, the blood came out over the shawl and turned my two hands red. Reminded that I had a proven cure for this, I rushed to get my special sack where I had loaded my herbal medicine and chose the one for bleeding. I mixed it with water, made very thick paste which I piled on top of the cut as he squirmed with the burning sensation.

Still kneeling down, I looked up to see his reaction and our eyes met for the first time. As he kept looking at me, I was drawn as if under the influence of a powerful spell, mesmerized by that magnificent splendour with a magnetic charisma of a fierce warrior, a wise leader and a passionate lover, all in one. As I remained frozen, it felt like time had stopped. First, I was unsure whether this was fear or attraction. But it was the latter. Yes, I had fallen in love.

The bleeding slowed down to a trickle; then stopped completely, as my husband looked incredulous over my immediate success. Next, I looked around the room and was delighted to find water in a pot, of which he drank with gusto. I then cleaned up the room, leaving no traces of our scheme. Not knowing what to say, I finally mumbled,

*"I pray to St. Tekle-Haimanot that this will have no effect on your health."*

Although I had spent a full day and half a night next to my husband, this was the first sentence I uttered to him. Upon hearing this, Lemma Tessema approached me, took my hands again, and held them tight against his chest, leaving bloody marks on his shirt.

"*Thank you. True to our vow, you stopped my bleeding with your wedding shawl. If nothing else, I hope to give you happiness,*" he said.

The time had finally come to report to the mother elders who were still outside, eagerly awaiting the evidence of the virginity test. I could see he was in pain as he slowly limped toward the door, holding the carefully-wrapped cloth, blood-soaked as if "I had been hit by a bullet". Outside, he submitted the evidence to the representative of the group. Upon seeing the bloody cloth, the group went berserk, as women erupted into the age-old song,

*"Our faithful daughter! Our faithful daughter!*

*"Honour to father! Honour to husband!"*

Immediately, a messenger was sent to deliver the good news of honour to my family. The dancing and singing continued all night as the news of my virginity was circulated in and outside the tent.

Now that the ploy was successfully carried out, Lemma Tessema looked relieved as he showed me the outhouse. Here, I was reminded that what had just happened was only a temporary solution because the *encounter* had to take place at any cost. I then realized that it would not be too long before I would be the one bleeding. To my shock, I found myself almost wishing that I was done with it this night so this pesky fear would be behind me.

Back in our room, I found Lemma Tessema resting on a stool, nursing his bandaged wound. As soon as he saw me, he got up, took my hand and led me to the bed where a set of gifts was displayed.

"*But, you have already showered me with generous gifts which I received yesterday*," I protested.

"*St. Tekle-Haimanot is my witness; I will shower you with love and gifts for the rest of my life*," he replied, "*For tonight though, I have given you my word of honour that nothing will happen. You are safe. I want you to have a good night's sleep. I will be resting on the small bed next to you*," he assured me.

Suspecting a surprise attack, I kept one eye open throughout the night, and jumped up every time I heard a movement. Lemma Tessema kept his word.

I started my married life with a week-long honeymoon. This being a period of recovery, *encounters* were forbidden so the bride could heal from her wound. Throughout the week, our cottage was filled with visitors who streamed in and out to congratulate my husband for marrying a faithful virgin while satisfying their curiosity about the much talked about beauty of Siqualla. Every day, I was kept busy by young girls who were selected to keep me company. Mostly my age, some were soon to be married and therefore full of questions,

"*We heard that the cloth was soaked with blood, he must have been wild,*

*"Hope you did not lose too much blood,*

*"Did you put up a fight at all?*

*"Are you still in pain? Does it hurt when you walk?*

*"Pity us; we are yet to go through all this."*

In reply, I kept repeating what I was told by my husband, "*Thank God, it is now behind me.*"

Throughout our honeymoon, we did not have a single moment of privacy. Yet, every time I turned around, I caught my husband watching me from a distance, sometimes with deep love, other times with a burning desire. On those occasions, I felt a nice, warm feeling all over my body, but I managed to hide it successfully, thanks to the tricks taught me by the Siqualla mothers. The fear of the *encounter* which I suspected was going to happen during the honeymoon also worked against my feeling any joy.

During the rare private hours, often late in the evening, Lemma Tessema always held my hands against his chest, saying, "*Please, Almaz, get a good night's sleep. I promise I will not harm you,*" and headed toward the small bed at the corner of the room. On the last night of our honeymoon, Lemma Tessema put my two hands against his chest.

"*Almaz,*" he said, "*Our honeymoon has come to an end and I must go back to work tomorrow. We come from two blessed families; your father gave us half of his livestock; your brothers built our cottage and we received a plot of land from my parents.*

*"We will use my monthly wage to hire helping hands. You will no longer go to the river to fetch water or to the bush to collect wood. Never, as long as I am alive! Instead, you will begin your studies next week, with my help.*

*"Now, before I ask you to go to your bed, I would like to hear you say my name for the first time. Please, Almaz."*

Overcome by this powerful affection, I choked with tears as I said, "*Lemma Tessema*" in a rather quivering voice. Upon hearing his name, he helped me get up, gathered me with his two hands, circled my arms around his neck and held me tight against his entire body. I rested my head on his chest where I could hear his heart beat like an African drum. Filled with pristine love, we merged into one. The temperature soared as if we were set on fire and we melted on to each other. It was here that I felt his thing stand up. Suddenly, he let go, saying, "*Please, go to sleep now. I promise I will not harm you.*"

Empowered by this beautiful love, I gradually became a happy wife, managing my married life with great enthusiasm. Thanks to my multitude of skills, I became a valuable member of the extended family, cooking, baking, weaving, and brewing. I welcomed every assignment and delivered good results, giving great relief to my mother-in-law and pride to my father-in-law.

I shared my knowledge of keeping food fresh, minimizing wood consumption and cooking food that was both tasty and nutritious. I demonstrated the different ways to weave a basket, spin cotton, ferment drink and preserve herbs. I gladly shared my herbal medicine for nausea, diarrhoea, fever, constipation, bleeding and headache. Within days, news went around about the jewel who was transforming Lemma Tessema's family. I could not have been prouder.

Gradually, my daily activities were divided into three: serving my in-laws, managing my marriage and following my studies. The endless demands from my in-laws did not deter me from keeping my husband as my first priority.

I planned our days ahead of time, keeping a meticulous list of meals for breakfast, lunch and dinner. I kept my husband pleasantly surprised by treating him to special dishes that he said were beyond his expectation.

With his teaching job and my service to the in-laws, our time was rather limited, but what we had was filled with joy as Lemma Tessema shared his stories, opening a completely new world to his peasant wife.

Of all my skills, my academic progress brought endless amazement to my husband who marvelled how far I had gone, considering that I was from the traditional "education camp." After giving me several tests in reading, writing, grammar and dictation, he concluded that I was at about grade five level. He then drew up a lesson that focused more on mathematics, science and literature.

As we say in Siqualla, I drank education like the fresh waters of the well. I handed in every assignment by the due date and passed every test with high marks. I asked questions which my teacher explained in great detail. I answered his questions correctly, always triggering deep affection which he expressed with a strong embrace and the assurance, "*Do not be afraid, Almaz, I said I will not harm you.*"

Enriched by care, respect and support for each other, love continued to flourish in our home, like a plant on a fertile land, under the warm sun, with abundant water. Every morning, we prayed for rain for the land and peace for its people. Before and after every meal, we thanked God for giving us our daily bread which we promised to share with the less fortunate. On Sundays, we went to church and received Christ's body and blood. We always carried food for the poor who wished us a blessed life filled with healthy children.

Slowly, I started opening up, sharing my childhood stories, sometimes weeping for no reason. This gave my husband an idea that I had missed home and needed to visit my family. To prepare for this occasion, he asked my in-laws to relieve me from my chores. Realizing that our visit was going to be another Siqualla event, Lemma Tessema insisted that I prepare everything necessary for a huge reception. The famous hair dresser was brought in to plait my hair and he helped me choose the best of the dresses. Love must have done something to my system; I glowed like the Siqualla stars on a cloudless night.

Indeed, our visit was like a second wedding, filled with joy and laughter, food and drink, music and dance. Every member of the extended family was invited back while neighbours simply turned up to spend the day, an evening or a night. A true mark of Siqualla, generosity was in abundance, as every visitor brought food and drink that lasted throughout the visit, creating surplus that was distributed among the poor. Somewhat mellowed, my father regained his usual excitement as he kept telling everyone,

*"The good Lord is still here. He has not abandoned us. Unlike us, God is patient; He does not rush. He does not hasten. The good Lord does not cut short. He will answer all our prayers, but in due time."*

After three days of bliss, it was time to bid farewell to Siqualla where we had been made to feel like King Solomon and the Queen of Sheba. As we were leaving, my father whispered into my ear that my husband had left a large sum of money for the family to help fill the absence of a much valued daughter.

As we made the trip back, Lemma Tessema said a lot about our visit, but not a word about his generosity. So, we barely entered home when I came right behind him, circled my arms around his waist, hid my face in his back and expressed my gratitude, "*Father told me about your generous gift. May St. Tekle-Haimanot reward you back.*"

Delighted by this unexpected display of affection, Lemma Tessema was encouraged to take a bold action. Still holding my hands, he turned around slowly so as to face me, then held my face with two hands and planted an affectionate kiss right on my forehead. This was my very first kiss from my husband. My heart accelerated as I hid my face in his chest, ashamed of what I had just caused him to do. He simply said, "*I will not harm you, Almaz. Please do not be afraid of me.*"

In our society, the transition from a girl child to a child bride was a period of trial. The beginning of married life was the time for brides to demonstrate their worth to society by proving their ability to bear children. A few weeks after the wedding night, a bride would be expected to share the happy news of pregnancy with her mother-in-law, "*Mother, you are to be blessed with a grandson*."

If this news was delayed, she would be asked, "*Have you been visited by our beloved Virgin Mariam*?" meaning have you conceived? To answer, "*Not yet*" was the most frightening prospect for every bride who would first be criticized, then suspected of infertility and finally subjected to a divorce.

Mine was a happy life. I cherished the times my husband was home and looked forward to sitting next to him, as he held my hands, checking for cuts and bruises, a result of the chores at his parents'. As we sat next to each other, he reminisced about his school days in Addis Ababa, telling me how he had been tormented by city boys for the rural way he talked, walked and dressed. He said that his only revenge was his academic lead against every student on every subject.

I also shared my story as a motherless child, raised by men who never saw me sleeping. Lemma Tessema acknowledged that this was one of the practices he was determined to change. It was here that he shared his vision for our future:

that I would be a teacher, like him, and lead a school for girls. He said that he was in a hurry to see this day and this was why our evenings were entirely devoted to reading, writing, studying and questions and answers.

At the end of my lesson, before heading toward our separate beds, we always enjoyed a magical moment of pristine love as we embraced affectionately, our bodies merged into one burning carving with my good-night kiss on the forehead. It always ended with my husband's solemn vow never to harm me.

One day, an idea came to me to host the extended family, colleagues and friends of my husband. We set the day to coincide with the anniversary of St. Tekle-Haimanot and I shared my plan as to what and how to prepare for the occasion. Lemma Tessema, though touched by my offer, seemed worried about the amount of work, so he insisted that his sisters give me a hand, an offer I gladly accepted.

Ahead of time, I prepared the ingredients, spices and herbs necessary for the food and drink to be served. For drinks I chose the popular honey mead which I fermented to the right level so that it was pleasing to the palate, but harmless to the system. On the eve, I baked injera[5] and a sheep was slaughtered to prepare the different dishes.

I started with the popular *dulet*[6], prepared with chopped tripe, kidney, mixed with onion, pepper, green chilli and spiced butter, barely cooked in medium heat. Next, I prepared *sega wot*[7] with lamb meat cut into small cubes, flavoured with

---

5 Ethiopian flat bread made from Teff.

6 Eaten raw or semi raw.

7 Spiced meat stew.

onion, garlic, ginger, cayenne pepper, spiced butter and a variety of herbs. I also made *alicha wot*.[8]

In addition, we slaughtered a few chickens which I cut up into twelve pieces each, washed thoroughly and cooked with a variety of spices. A chicken dish is never served without eggs. So, into this dish, I added several boiled eggs. I then baked three kinds of bread: *hibest* baked with steam, *ambasha*, baked on clay oven and *dabo*, flavoured with a variety of spices.

When the invited guests arrived, I retreated to the kitchen where I remained throughout the evening, keeping my sisters-in-law almost idle as I buzzed around like a bee, discharging one task after another with great ease. Treated to a memorable evening, the guests poured their praises to my father-in-law who, they said, had brought a jewel to the family. At the end of the evening, Father-in-Law stood up to say his blessings which he ended with good wishes for "a happy life, filled with healthy children."

Lemma Tessema hardly waited for the last guest to leave when he joined me in the kitchen where he found me resting, tired, but relieved to have fulfilled my promise. There was something different about his demeanour that night as he took my two hands, palms up and kissed them one after another, many times over, in an expression of his gratitude.

He then moved on to give me my very first kisses on the eyes, cheeks, nose, and then my lips which he barely touched, but enough to give me a jolt. I was warned by village women that a kiss on the lips was always a prelude to something bigger. So, I pushed him aside and started heading out of the kitchen. He pulled me back, saying,

---

8 Alicha wot is made with onion, garlic, venison meat, spiced butter, turmeric, and chillies.

*"My beloved, on our wedding day, I could almost not breathe when I saw you were so beautiful. It was here that my heart was filled with a commitment to protecting you with my life. If I have crossed the line tonight, it is because I am overwhelmed by your love. Rest assured; I will never do anything that harms you."*

Hearing this assurance filled me with confidence that I was indeed safe with my husband. Immediately, I relented and went right back to my favourite spot, his chest, where I always rested my head, listened to his heart beat and enjoyed his body temperature. Again, we parted to go to our separate beds.

It was now six months, two weeks and four days since our wedding. On this particular afternoon, I was busy working on my assignment when Lemma Tessema walked in, shaking like a lonely tree on a windy day, complaining, "*I am not feeling well, my beloved.*" I cried out with terror when I saw that he was burning like a torch and drenched in sweat as if fished out of a river. I refused to let go, asking what was wrong until he assured me that this was malaria and it would go away as soon as he took his pills.

I was relieved to know that this was something I had a cure for, which I insisted he try. He agreed reluctantly. I took charge. First, I led him to my bed which I said was more comfortable for someone in his condition. Immediately, from my collection, I took this concoction of herbs known for its immediate and effective cure of malaria.

After soaking it in water, I squeezed the mixture hard to produce several reddish droplets which he snorted until he started coughing. Next, I added more water to the remaining droplets and asked him to drink the mixture, not minding the bitter taste. Lastly, I smeared his entire chest with the thick paste and covered him with layers of bed clothing "*to sweat the fever out*," as we say in Siqualla.

I then set about to make coffee; a serene ceremony designed by our foremothers to create an environment that soothes aching hearts and heals ailing bodies. First, I roasted the green coffee beans on a charcoal burner, producing an aromatic smoke that filled the house, welcoming the spirits of good health. Then, I ground the coffee and mixed it with water and let the mixture boil in a clay coffee pot until it was brewed to the right taste. Last, I burnt incense and prayed,

"*Our compassionate Lord, You who knows our inside thoughts and feelings, forgive me for not showing it openly, but You do know that I am in love with my husband. Please cure him for me for I see no life without him.*"

I kissed the floor and wiped my tears. When I went to serve the coffee, I found Lemma Tessema fast asleep. Quietly, I climbed up, lay down next to him, my hand on his forehead, feeling the heat wave that was burning his body. When I finally woke up after several hours, it was dark at night; my coffee ceremony was incomplete, with coffee pot and cups all over the floor; the incense burnt out, and my husband asking for a sip of water.

I jumped up, apologized profusely for my behaviour and rushed to get him water. If he had been surprised to find me lying next to him, he did not say for he simply drank the water, thanked me and went right back to sleep. As much as I wanted to restrain myself, I still had this strong desire to be next to him, feel his body and share his pain. So, I remained with him till the next morning when we were both woken up by the regular crow.

Seeing that I was lying outside the pile of bed clothes, he lifted each layer one by one, made an opening and asked me to join him. He put the pile back on both of us and said,

*"Of all the gifts God has given us, love is unique in its power to heal pain. My beloved, you cured me from this deadly disease not with your herbs, but with your love. I tasted true happiness yesterday when you touched me for the first time both on my forehead and chest. You are not an accidental bride of an arranged marriage; you are my precious gift from God."*

He then asked me to tell him in my own words that I loved him. In response, I expressed my inner most feelings for the first time:

*"Six months ago, I did not know you, nor did I care for you. I had only feelings of fear towards you. How it happened, I cannot say. But, today, I admit that I am truly in love with you. The love that God said we should have for each other is the love I have for you.*

*"I long for you when you are away. My heart jumps with delight when you are home and I feel sensations all over my body every time you hold me. Your love is flowing in my blood, reaching every part of my body.*

*"No woman has ever loved as I am loving you. The bloody marks I left on your shirt are the true words of my love for all eternity."*

Stunned by this candid confession, Lemma Tessema was rendered speechless. Instead, he simply slipped his left arm right under and pulled me with his right arm until I lined up against his entire frame, head to toe. Next, he circled my left arm around his waist and we celebrated this historic moment of oneness when our love reached the peak of all human feelings. He then said,

*"Now that I know you do love me, I would like to tell you something. I am so afraid of hurting you that we will have to wait a bit longer before we engage in the encounter."*

Bashful and puzzled, I promptly broke his gaze, nodding my head in agreement. He then unleashed endless kisses all over my face, as I gave him the freedom to reach where he wished. As usual, he stopped, promising,

*"I will never harm you, my sweet bride. I will indeed give my life for you."*

Later that morning, after giving him the second round of my herbal medicine, I prepared a special breakfast and suggested that we invite his mother to join us for the coffee ceremony. Agreed, he settled down, looking forward to an enjoyable morning with his wife and mother.

When I told Mother-in-Law that Lemma Tessema was unwell and invited her to join us for coffee, she brought up the inevitable subject.

*"I want to hear about your illness, Almaz, not your husband's,"* she said. *"When will you have morning sickness? It is now six months. Haven't you been visited by our beloved St. Mariam?"*

*"Not yet, Mother,"* I answered, clenching my teeth to stop the tremor that shook me.

Throughout the coffee ceremony, what she said played in my ears over and over, leaving me oblivious to the conversation between son and mother. My fear grew to an unimaginable height as I asked myself,

*"What if he decides never to know me?*

*"What if I am now too old to have a child?*

*"What if we are to divorce?*

*"What if he stops loving me?"*

I took full responsibility for my unreasonable fear that prevented my husband from performing the *encounter* on our wedding night. Next, I blamed him, calling him unmanly and spineless for bleeding himself instead of forcing his wife. Then it was my mother-in-law whom I criticized for meddling in our life, calling her a marriage destroyer.

As soon as she left, I told Lemma Tessema that his mother was worried that I had not been visited by our Lady Mariam. I said that she had indeed been patient long enough and it was time to present her with good news. Gently, he said,

*"This is time for education, not for children. We have time for a family."*

*"I was not sent here for education, I am here to have children,"* I answered back.

*"A child cannot have a child,"* he replied, "You are *not yet ready to be a mother."*

This came across to me as meaning that I could not conceive. Aware that infertility was the most serious blame on women, I hit back with anger,

*"I think you are the one who has been unable to perform; not me."*

*"That is not true,"* he said, *"I feel like blowing up every time I touch you and you are blaming me for not performing?"*

He then proceeded to explain the consequences of a premature encounter.

*"Almaz, do you really understand what an encounter is? Do you? You see, my beloved, our culture is obsessed with the*

*chastity of girls. So, we have invented a life-time punishment called female circumcision which, in reality, is the mutilation of the female organ in order to kill off the desire for intimacy. Imagine, the entire female population in Siqualla is missing a body part and no one seems to care. But, I do because I love you.*

*"While abstinence is the preferred option in places like Siqualla where health and social services are absent, there is no justification to mutilate the entire female population simply because society has decided that women and girls are bearers of family honour.*

*"What you and I are enjoying is genuine, pristine love. If I touch you, I will certainly enjoy enormous pleasure, but you will go through such a pain that you will start to see me as someone who hurt you. I will not allow this to happen to you. You are the love of my life to whom I gave my word of honour inside a church.*

*"Then, there is this thing called fistula. If you get pregnant at such a young age, you will suffer fistula which will leave you a tragic human being for the rest of your life. Since you are too young to conceive, you can easily develop fistula which is caused after days of pushing a baby that does not fit through the birth canal, causing severe vaginal and rectal damage.*

*"This means you will become incontinent, unable to control both urine and feces. You will drain waste permanently, producing an offensive smell that will surround you day and night. If you do not believe me, there is a hospital in Addis Ababa, run by Doctor Catherine Hamelin who is treating hundreds of young women like you, who suffered fistula after their marriage when they were forced to engage in a premature encounter.*

*"Believe me; a woman with fistula is shunned by her husband, her in-laws and yes, by her parents. My love for you is such that I am simply unable to take such a risk.*

*"Third, while you have amazed me with your academic progress, you are not yet ready to be a teacher. My beloved, you need a few more years of schooling so you can take up an occupation and become self-sufficient. With education, you can see the fruits of your labour when young girls like you start to read, write and go on to become teachers. This will give you a purpose in life.*

*"This means we will have to wait for some time before we engage in the encounter. I am willing to prove my love for you by waiting for as long as it takes. Are you?"*

I had just been presented with three impossibilities; an old, stubborn culture I could not change, the threat of a frightening disease, and a beautiful love that filled my heart to the brim. Suddenly, I was overwhelmed by an imaginary strong stench of feces reeking from my body, and I felt like running away from myself. Hopeless and defeated, I reached out to my husband, but only to find that he too was drained of all feelings. The drum in his chest was beating no more. The fire that consumed our bodies was gone and the hard thing I always felt between his legs was paralyzed. This was the first hour of our long trial.

The next day, cured from his malaria, my husband took off to work, promising to be home early to help me with my studies. I rushed to my in-laws', wondering whether the plan for the day was to cook, bake, brew or weave. Instead, I was received by Mother-in-Law, looking rather impatient.

*"Almaz, for the last six months, I showered you with blessings for a happy life, filled with healthy children,"* she said.

*"Since your wedding night, I have been dreaming, hoping and planning for a grandson for whom I have already chosen a name and identified the family for a prospective wife.*

*"I had missed out on much motherly happiness when my son was taken away. For fifteen years, I longed for this boy every day. I think I now deserve some belated happiness as the grandmother of his son. Our son has brought us great honour with his schooling; so his name must be kept for posterity.*

*"But you made sure that this was not going to be. Almaz, are you aware of the deep sadness you have caused this family? Your husband has confided in me of his immense love for you. But what is love in a childless home?"*

For a moment, I wondered whether these were mere words or spears with poison ends that pierced my heart and came out the other side. Then, there was the painful realization that I was no longer "the jewel of the family" who brought beauty, fame and transformed my in-laws. Instead, I was now a barren woman who caused deep grief to the family of my good husband.

When she was done, I quietly slipped out of the room and headed toward the kitchen where I was given several tasks which I performed with great care to demonstrate that I was still valuable to the family. Crushed, with a bleeding heart, I finally headed home to attend to my studies.

Back from work, if my husband noticed something amiss, he did not say so, he still looked cheerful and madly in love. First he checked my hands for cuts and bruises, then proceeded to embrace me, kiss me, compliment me for my beauty, admire me for my studies and thank me for serving the family.

This was my moment. I swam with joy and flew in excitement. All the spears that had pierced me earlier melted away one by one and my heart overflowed with joy. I decided to shield him from the sad story of the morning with his mother. When we finished our evening studies, I was presented with a special request,

"...to *come to your bed as I am still feverish with the malaria*."

I gladly accepted this lie and we spent another glorious night next to each other. Early in the morning, we were surprised by Mother-in-Law who said that she had come to discuss a serious matter. First, she addressed my husband:

*"Lemma, my son, you know that you are not an ordinary person or an average citizen. We have known this since your birth because of the unique gifts God has given you. Because you were His choice, He also brought the Good Samaritan into your life to give you an opportunity for urban schooling. Again, God gave you the courage to abandon the comforts of city life and return to your rural roots. Because of you, today Siqualla is on its way to civilization.*

*"Even though it seemed odd for a schooled man to marry a peasant girl, your father kept his word in marrying you to Almaz. While we have no regrets about that, we shall never accept that you remain childless.*

*"Your father and I are grieving over the news that Almaz is infertile. A young bride who loves her husband always conceives on the first encounter. If a bride cannot conceive at fifteen, it is a sign that there is a serious problem.*

*"I admit that the love between you two cannot be measured in human terms. But, in the absence of children, this love is only a fickle, a temporary desire for the pleasure of the flesh."*

She then addressed me.

*"Almaz, I assure you that there is no history of infertility on our side,"* she started, *"Praise be to our beloved Mariam, she has blessed us abundantly. So, we have decided that you must go back to your family at once and seek treatment for infertility."*

Grief weighing in his heart and anger painted all over his face, my husband responded.

*"Mother, I love you, I honour you and I admire you. You are the glue who held our family together in good and bad times. You are a woman of courage who sacrificed a five-year old child to urban life because you believed schooling would bring a bright future to him, to our family and the community. And your sacrifices are paying off to the benefit of all Siqualla. But, today you have hurt me profoundly.*

*"If you must know the truth, Almaz is still a virgin. I have not touched her on our wedding night, during the honeymoon or in the last months. She is as she has come. The virginity evidence I submitted to mother elders was stained with my own blood, not hers.*

*"I am so afraid of hurting her that I had to shed my own blood for her sake. I have given her my word of honour that I will not harm her and, if need be, I am ready to die for her. This is how much I love my wife.*

*"So, here is my response. From the moment I laid eyes on my bride, I knew that we were meant for each other. So our love is not a temporary desire of the flesh; it is a true gift of God. I love her and I cannot live without her. I will not allow her to leave me; so she is not going anywhere.*

*"Almaz does not need any treatment; she will conceive when she is ready. Right now, she is not a woman yet; she is just*

*a child. Whatever God has in store for us, we will die husband and wife, with or without children."*

On his way out, he approached her, knelt down and kissed her knees to ask for forgiveness. She touched his head to say, "*I forgive you.*"

The next day, both parents arrived at dawn, armed with an ultimatum, a well prepared case which Father-in-Law presented, saying that it was non-negotiable.

*"Son, we are here to discuss the tragedy that has befallen this family. Please bear with us.*

*"You two seem to think that our culture is a haphazard collection of beliefs and practices with no meaning or purpose. In reality, everything we do in this society has a value for this society. So, you must see us from where we are, Lemma, not from where you stand.*

*"Our values have grown out of a long tradition that sustained us for generations and we intend to keep them. You cannot pick and drop them willy-nilly as if they were pebbles. So, please spare us your schooled judgment. It may not look good to you, but our culture is right in our eyes.*

*"This brings me to this family's utmost concern, that of children – your children. Son, when the British invaded our nation, our valiant leader, Emperor Tewodros, retreated to the Magdella Plateau from where he tried to stop the advancing enemy.*

*"When he realized that the British had the upper hand, he shot himself dead because he could not bring himself to see his people under a foreign rule. The British abandoned their original plan of colonization, but, on their way out, they plundered our nation.*

*"While we had lost much during this plunder, it was the abduction of our prince heir who they took to their country that left a lasting scar on our nation. To this day, we continue to grieve over this loss. Why? In our society, children are not born to husband and wife. Every child is born to society. Here, children are not the accidental outcome of an encounter; there is always a higher purpose to having them.*

*"We do not choose not to have them. You must understand that in our society we do not engage in the encounter to enjoy the fleeting sensation of the flesh. The sole purpose of an encounter is to have a child. Had there been a different way of producing babies, the encounter would have no place in our society. It would be irrelevant.*

*"When God created us, He did not say go and enjoy sex[9]. He told us to multiply and fill the earth. This encounter that you so disdain is God's gift. Admittedly, women do carry the heavier weight because they, not men, were chosen by our beloved Mariam to be the bearers of this gift. So, if your wife experiences some discomfort due to the encounter, pregnancy or child birth, nature has its own way of healing her pain.*

*"My son, our society has been in existence for centuries and no one has ever defied our culture in such a flagrant way as you two did. By staining the virginity test cloth with your own blood, you misled an entire village into believing that you consummated the marriage.*

*"Lemma, you might find us slow, uninspiring and dull, but we do have the same capacity to think, to love, and to feel pain or to enjoy happiness. God has given us the same feelings that you claim to be solely yours. You have no monopoly of love of or respect for women. God is our witness; we never did and*

9 While encounter is viewed as God's gift, sex is seen as something dirty.

*never will plan to harm them. We may be backward in many things, but lack of love is not one of them.*

*"As much as we are known for respect and generosity, we are unforgiving against those who disrespect our culture and defy our values. It is, therefore, with much regret that I inform you that my family has decided to disown you and your wife.*

*"The ties between you two and this family are severed and will remain so as long as I am walking on this earth. You will no longer carry my name, live on my land and enjoy the fruits of my labour. I forbid you to attend my funeral and condemn your presence at my death bed.*

*"The same goes with every member of my family, including your mother, all siblings and their children. This is our ultimate decision. I bid you farewell."*

When they walked out, my husband fell on his knees and cried like a child. Having seen his love and respect for his family, I knew that this was his moment of loss and I grieved quietly with guilt.

# Chapter Six

In the early hours of the next day, my father, accompanied by four sons, arrived in response to a request from my father-in-law who, they said, had told them the full story and asked for help in facilitating our move out of his homestead. To my relief, my father offered us a place to stay, a face-saving offer which we accepted with gratitude.

As a sign of our penance, we agreed to leave behind all our livestock. The wedding gift from my father had now become a gift of forgiveness to my in-laws, a peace-making offer commonly exchanged among adversaries. We cleared out the newly built cottage, packed our personal belongings and headed toward a new life.

Except for love, our marriage was now bankrupt, tarnished with dishonour, shame, disrespect, gossip and dislocation. As I marched toward yet another uncertainty, I marvelled how fast we had come down from a once admired couple to two vile individuals. Socially, we became the same as those who stopped breathing. Of the two of us, my husband had died more because no man had ever suffered the fate of having to seek shelter at his in-laws.

My husband would be ridiculed as a coward who conspired to shelter his infertile wife at the expense of his own reputation. Village gossipers and comedians would invent demeaning nicknames, calling him the man who tampered with the virginity test. He would not be mentioned in the presence of children in case they would be poisoned by his evil influence.

In less than a single day, I witnessed the fall of a giant into nothingness. No amount of courage could hide the wound that my husband sustained in his pride.

Upon arrival in my father's homestead, we quietly slipped into our cottage where we took shelter from a warring society. While the education camp had proven to be more forgiving, it was not yet ready to lay out the welcome mat. I knew how badly we had sinned when not a single person turned up to utter a welcoming word or to extend a helping hand. And these were the same people who had feasted, danced and rejoiced at our wedding.

As we say in Siqualla, "*Once fallen, a majestic tree becomes the playground for ants and beetles.*" Once King Solomon and the Queen of Sheba, we were now two refugees hosted by a reluctant society. Next, we would be treated so badly that we would leave on our own volition, as we say in Siqualla,

"*Do not tell them, make them leave.*"

As if he read my mind, my husband comforted me, "*Almaz, if you feel unwelcome here, we can go to Addis Ababa where I can take a teaching job and you will attend school.*"

Hearing this, I decided to rise to the occasion as the wife of the man who fell from the highest high to the lowest low. Carefully, I introduced the subject, hoping that he still had some energy left to bear with me. Calling him beloved for the first time, I said that if we kept running from challenges, we would soon run out of asylum places.

"*My beloved husband,* you *have lost most of what you earned,*" I said, "*the love of your family and the respect of our society. This is no less than the loss of life. You cannot recover this loss merely by fighting your or my family because the entire old culture is our foe – and a formidable one."*

I reminded him that he was able to convince Siqualla into accepting education, health and justice systems for the first time not by breaking its rules but by opening its eyes. I then concluded, saying,

*"You must, once more, use education as your tool to bring about this change. This demands standing up, not running away."*

When I saw a slight nod of agreement, I was encouraged to go on,

"*My husband,*" I continued, "*a cultural war has been declared against you simply for refusing to harm the woman you love. I know of only Christ who died for love. My grief over your loss is as great as my determination to stand by your side until you regain your place in our community. So, I urge you to allow me to be with you as you fight this war because my love for you is just as deep, as genuine and as everlasting as yours for me.*"

As I said these words I felt a powerful passion, a desire for my husband and that magical moment of oneness with its healing qualities. How I wanted to be inside him, feeling warm and dizzy, tightly held against his body and my head resting on his pounding chest.

My husband, who always read my mind, knew at once that love had taken control of me. As I flew into his arms, he welcomed me with a huge embrace and, as if afraid of losing each other, we merged into one ebony-mahogany carving.

Lemma Tessema had a gift of expressing love that was firm but gentle, strong but kind. He was generous with his feelings, but measured with his physical advances. He was neither overwhelming nor distant in his intimacy. This time, he was about to ease up his embrace when I refused to let go, holding my arms tighter around his waist. Taken aback, he started kissing me all over my face and, for the first time, I kissed him back, weeping as if I was reunited with a lost lover.

Surprised by this dramatic change, Lemma Tessema realized that my love for him had indeed become so powerful that it literally shattered the cultural barriers that had kept it prisoner. And he celebrated this moment of freedom. Every now and then, I caught him beaming a smile of victory that he had succeeded in bringing me to this level of intimacy.

When he noticed that I was going mad with desire, he seemed worried as to what else to do, beyond the new horizon we had reached tonight. Finally, he treated me to a sip of water and asked if he could tell me a story from a faraway land. He then led me to the rickety bed and lay next to me, stroking my hair gently and kissing me non-stop as if he knew I was too hungry to say "*Enough*."

As I comfortably rested my insane head on his chest, his hand on my forehead and my arms around his waist, he told me a story from a distant land, a story of love, and tragic death due to a family feud.

*"The people who invaded our nation and took our prince came from a country of outstanding people," he started, "One of these was Mr. William Shakespeare, the greatest writer who ever lived. I am now reminded of him because he wrote our story a long time ago, calling us Romeo and Juliet. Like Romeo and Juliet, we are young, in love and condemned to a sin we did not commit. But, unlike them, we will not die; our love shall triumph over evil."*

He promised that we would enjoy love for the rest of our life, and, at the same time, bring about a historic change in Siqualla, liberating women and girls from harmful cultural practices. Before he finished his story of our future, I phased into a beautiful dreamy sleep.

The next day, as we woke up to a new life, we looked at each other dazed, as if we did not know how we got to where we had come and unsure how to get out from where we ended. A frightening realization had set in. We were two individuals whose journey had taken the opposite path and we did not know how to turn it around.

At this very moment, we heard a loud commotion outside where, it seemed, some strangers were asking where to find us. Nearly homeless and at risk of losing the little we had, we both jumped up in panic and my husband stepped out to find out what was going on. A messenger sent by his family told Lemma Tessema that the herd of cattle we left behind was sent back because his father had declined our penance.

What we called *Kassa*[10] was never rejected in Siqualla. Ours would go down in history as the first to be turned down; which meant that our little, faint hope that we might one day receive forgiveness was now snuffed like a candle light.

This was when we truly understood that what we had done was not a mere rebellion against harmful cultural practices but something as grave as committing a murder. This was further explained by the messenger who was asked to deliver the livestock, along with the family's final word of parting as if we needed a reminder that Siqualla's Adam and Eve were expelled from paradise…forever.

10 A gift of forgiveness

We listened with a renewed sense of grief as the messenger read out the contents of the farewell letter which revealed that our penance could not heal the immense hurt suffered by the family and, indeed, the community at large. We were told that our deceitful act had shaken the very foundation of their trust, spread a cloud of doubt across the village and left a permanent stain of anger on every member of the extended family.

*"If you still believe that you are good people, we wish to remind you that a bad mistake is what distinguishes good people from bad,"* the letter concluded.

Seeing our disappointment, the elder took time to explain the complex nature of human relationships and how they were built, maintained and mended. We asked him to tell us why our penance did not work.

"*Because* you *treated your kassa as if it was a payment or a bribe so you could look good to others. Forgiveness is never sold or bought; it is earned through genuine remorse,"* he explained.

He told us that we only cared about our loss and never thought of the hurt we caused the community. He regretted the fact that we were still determined to maintain our position on women's issues even if this went against the long-standing values of the community.

This was true. We had indeed overlooked our own failings. Not once did we say, "*We hurt our people. We disrespected our elders. We defied our culture.*" Worse, we failed to recognize Siqualla's collective repulsion against deceit. Had Lemma Tessema told women elders, on our wedding night, that he would not perform the *encounter*, he would have been condemned, but with respect for standing up with courage.

It turned out; it was the worst thing we could have done. By keeping it secret, we ignited a village-wide rumour that the real reason was to hide my infertility, a curse that demanded a divorce.

Life in my father's homestead was like living on borrowed time with the on-going fear of an imminent expulsion. I remained secluded in our leaky, shaky cottage, except for the surreptitious visits by my father who came regularly to deliver our daily needs, always looking the reluctant visitor.

As for my husband, his happy days were quickly winding down, if not already over. When student absences increased overnight, it was evident that this was not a plague, rather a revolt against Lemma Tessema. Although my husband had asked to keep authorities out of this matter, the school issued a warning against absences without a valid reason. The effect was a quiet simmering resentment throughout the village, pushing the conflict from "Lemma Tessema against culture" to "government against people."

As I followed the steady escalation of our simple act into a revolt, I asked myself about me.

"*Who is this Almaz Tefera in the midst of turmoil? A culprit who willingly joined a traitor to defy an ancient culture? A comrade armed with a powerful love, recruited into a one-man revolution? A naïve peasant girl lured to push a society out of its comfort zone?*"

When I realized that I was indeed all of these, I saw two irreconcilable images of myself: a loyal wife seeking positive change vs. a renegade who chose a man over her society.

While my education remained our primary focus, we always made time for a serious dialogue about how we had started what looked like a movement. Guilt and regret always found their way into our conversation, testing our resolve. Yet, Lemma Tessema was never one to surrender. Rather, every Sunday he lamented the prospect of one more bride to be subjected to a pre-mature *encounter* with its potential effects of physical pain, mental anguish, demeaning virginity test, early pregnancy, fistula and, in the end, a poor, old woman with several poor children.

As days grew into weeks and months headed toward a year, Lemma Tessema grew impatient and started looking for different ways to speed up social change. On this particular evening, he told me that his hopes that the school camp would be an ally in his efforts to open Siqualla's eyes to the plight of its daughters were dashed. He was now convinced that we stood to win not by changing the attitudes of the school camp but by stirring the emotions of the education camp with its faith in God and reverence to our Virgin Mariam.

"*When it comes to women and girls,*" he said, "*both the school and education camps are equally blinded by cultural blinkers. What do you think, my beloved? Should we use the emotions of the heart or the reasoning of the mind? I need your advice,*" he asked.

Surprised by the sudden change of strategy, I disagreed with my husband. I told him that the education camp was not entirely built on blocks of sentiments that one could easily stir with stories of the female plight. It was also governed by a well-founded system of reasoning that followed its own logic.

I pointed out that the education camp was also aware that our much revered Mariam was a fifteen-year old virgin when she was blessed with Christ. His own mother had her first child before she saw her first monthly flower[11]. My own mother successfully gave birth to four children before she died having me at age twenty.

I also cautioned against creating an artificial boundary between the two schools which were like water from the same river. I explained this further that while he belonged to the school camp, he always came back to his peasant wife and his students returned to families filled with people from the education camp. I then warned him.

*"Your concern about women's place in society could be seen as insincere, something you have raised because you have run out of real issues. Be patient, my beloved, you will soon be joined by someone who sees your vision, walks your walk and is ready to share your sacrifices. We must give education a chance."*

In response, Lemma Tessema agreed that the best tool for change was education.

*"As we say in Siqualla, to kill an idea is to blow out the candle that lights a dark alley. You are right, my bride, I agree with your conclusion and support your suggestion. Let's give education a chance."*

But he did not entirely buy my story about the Virgin Mariam and our two mothers. He said that for every girl who escaped the debilitating effects of early, forced or child marriage, there was a child bride hidden in a private home, out of community sight, suffering from fistula.

*"Almaz, we must stop this epidemic now. I cannot wait till next Sunday,"* he concluded.

---

[11] In Siqualla, menstrual period is called "yewer ababa", meaning a flower that blossoms every month.

As he said this, there was a tone of urgency in his voice and a look of unflinching determination in his face. At one point, he looked as if he was facing a deadly enemy, ready to strike a fatal blow. This brought tears of anger into my eyes, but I refused to give in, pushed my tears back and came up with a rather drastic suggestion. Feeling resolute, I asked a question.

"*How about a government ban against harmful cultural practices? This would be similar to the mandatory registration of girls that was imposed in your school when the government took over the education system,*" I reminded him.

My husband who saw the merits of my suggestion was surprised by how far I was prepared to go to stop this scourge. But, he was not ready to give up on education. All along, Lemma Tessema had suspected that I did not truly understand the root causes of the entrenched inequality between women and men in our society. He started to educate me how women fared in our society and why. To bring this point home, my husband used my own fate as an example.

"*Do you remember how fast you became unimportant in the eyes of my parents when they suspected you of infertility?*"

As he continued with his explanation, I felt like a membrane that kept my vision blurred had been peeled off my eyes. Suddenly, the barriers seemed too obvious. I was revolted to see that women's worth was actually determined by their role in procreation and that their very existence was justified exclusively on their ability to bear children.

Indeed, how did I not see that men were prepared to assume authority, to become leaders and to make decisions, including decisions concerning women's lives? In contrast, women were trained to become faithful subjects who obeyed men's orders. Within families, fathers were expected to rule and mothers to obey. A husband always made decisions while a wife fulfilled his wishes. Sons were allowed to choose what they wanted and daughters were required to accept what they were given.

When I asked why women did not object this unfair treatment, he said that it was because they were made to believe that their place in society was a destiny chosen them by God Himself and not an outcome of a social system. He told me that the beautiful gift of childbirth was turned into a weapon, creating conditions that sustained the inequality between women and men.

As well, women were constrained by archaic cultural values that limited their freedom to examine, explore and stand against unfair social systems. As a result, women and girls had no choice but to develop the mental and physical strength that enabled them to live with fatigue, pain, hardship, disease, and poverty as if these were integral to being a woman.

Beaming the smile that always melted my heart, he then spoke about us.

*"By my decision to produce the false virginity evidence, I have put you in a dangerous position because the community is now convinced that we were trying to hide your infertility. This hurts me to my bones. Nonetheless, we have created a dangerous precedent for this community.*

*"From here on, every time a virginity test result is submitted to mother elders, they will be forced to ask, "Is it really hers? Or is it his blood? No one had imagined that Siqualla would see this day. While there is still much to do, you and I have already accomplished something historic."*

Coming back to my suggestion of government ban, my husband observed that a government intervention against forced, early or child marriage might work, but it should be the last resort because, all by itself, it was bound to fail. He worried that, in the absence of education, a government measure could drive the practice underground and every girl in the village would turn eighteen overnight.

"*We should be careful not to lose track of the fight at such a critical time. As you said, let's give education a chance, my beloved,*" he concluded.

Now nearly a year into our marriage, our love had reached a new level of maturity, giving us joy in the present and hope for the future. Barely fifteen and twenty-two, we still enjoyed the giddy moments of racing hearts, sizzling bodies and the explosive desire for each other. My fear of the *encounter* had slowly disappeared and, in its place, I was filled with an intoxicating passion for my husband every time he held me.

Now that our love was reinforced by trust and confidence, my husband's assurances that he would not harm me became unnecessary. For me, the safest place was now the rickety, squeaky bed where I lay next to him, as he read me poetry, short stories, history books, until I slowly entered a beautiful sleep that lasted till the next morning. As my confidence grew, I woke up every morning, feeling an immense pride as his wife.

Sensing that ours was going to be a long and lonely journey, Lemma Tessema worried about my mental health and deliberately brought up happy stories about our future. In this story of hope, my husband predicted that we would be blessed with two children: a boy to be named after my father and a daughter after his mother. Our family would live in a big Siqualla home with several extra rooms which we used for evening class for girls.

As we grew older, we would be known as two exemplary teachers who changed the place of women in society. He also said that the story of our love would become a subject of books, music, poetry and play. He always ended his day dreaming with the last years "*of a very old man and a beautiful bride.*"

For me, this was simply a tale of fantasy, too good to be true for a couple that had nothing, but love. Always optimistic, my husband convinced me with a sound logic, an affectionate hug and one or two sweet kisses that we would definitely have a happy future.

Gradually, whenever I found myself alone, I got into the habit of closing my eyes and daydreaming about Lemma Tessema's vision of our future. In the first scene, I saw my two children, sitting next to each other, sharing a book, the girl helping her brother. Next, I saw several young girls, back from school, in and out of the extra rooms in our house, busy with their studies.

The third was about our love. My heart raced every time I saw this scene. His hair, grey on the temples, and my face wrinkled around my eyes, my husband and I were still filled with intense love as I wrapped myself around him and said,

"*I demand a kiss just like in the days of our youth, Father of my Children.*"

Quickly, he held my two hands and planted his magnetic kiss on my forehead sending fever throughout my body.

"*Yes, Mother of my Children, with all my love. And, one more for me, please,*" as he offered another affectionate kiss.

When I woke up from these daydreams, I always felt a chill all over my body with the realization that this was a far-fetched wish woven by a husband desperate to save his wife from insanity. On this particular day, I wept like a widow who lost the love of her life, pleading with God's ardent servant:

*"Our much loved St. Tekle-Haimanot, I was raised to honour God and obey his commandments. I have now become a disgraced bride, suspected of infertility, disowned by my in-laws, distanced by my family and condemned by society.*

*"Dear Saint: On my wedding night, I wept from the bottom of my heart because I believed that I was with someone who was going to harm me. That night, I feared Lemma Tessema for my very life as if he was my worst enemy.*

*"I now see that you have united me with a good man. With him, I feel safe, I feel protected and I feel loved. My fear and distrust have been replaced by happiness. I am truly and deeply in love with my husband.*

*"Today, I pray for my husband whose sin was to love his wife, for whom he had shed his blood, lost his status and, if need be, is prepared to die. I plead with you to bless him to be my life companion, and to be the father of our children.*

*"Above all, protect our love from anger, impatience and misunderstanding as we go through this difficult life. Amen."*

# Chapter Seven

With time, we adapted to this grim life of absent friends and undeclared enemies. Time had passed with little progress, until one day when something unexpected happened. On this day, we received a surprise visit from my father and three of my brothers who had decided to end their boycott. The fourth decided to opt out. With this day of reconciliation, the stars were about to shine upon us, heralding happier days for the rest of our life.

Already committed to prospective wives, my three brothers were expected to be married off one after the other, but they told my husband that they had decided to follow his example and delay the wedding. They vowed to support us even if they felt that what we did was deceitful, shameful and cowardly.

"*Brother-in-Law, we shall not continue to be bystanders, watching you from a distance as you put your name, your future and your life to the test for the sake of our sister,*" they told my husband.

Finally, three serious, genuine comrades declared their support for our cause. Yet, Lemma Tessema was not too keen to recruit. He asked questions, probed their motives and tested their commitment. To make sure that they understood what was involved, he first explained the negative effects of the prevailing inequality between men and women. He then told them that this was not only about their sister, but also for every girl and woman in our society.

This was also the time my husband had been waiting to tell my family the truth about the virginity test story which was converted into a completely different tale.

"*In spite of the rumour that is spreading throughout the village,*" he told them, "*Almaz is not infertile. I assure you that she is still the virgin girl given me by this family. And I refuse to destroy her simply to be accepted by society. She will have children when she is ready. So, as you can see, I am not a criminal. My only sin was to protect my wife from harmful cultural practices.*"

My brothers looked unconvinced; even so, they vowed again to stand by his side. While not impressed by their fervour, my husband was convinced about their honesty. Even if the recruits lacked knowledge, our force had now grown by two fold.

A true educator, my husband had a unique gift of opening eyes, minds and hearts. In a rather short time, he succeeded in educating my brothers, developed an alliance with a common purpose and instilled strong discipline among his recruits. This amazing visionary who transformed Siqualla into a place of hope and liberated my heart from a cultural colony was now building a committed team of comrades.

Gradually, our cottage became a lively meeting place where strategies were discussed while I hosted the company, serving coffee to keep the mind sharp and the night long. Amidst serious dialogue, heated debate, light jokes and roaring laughter, my husband made sure that I remained a full and active participant, constantly asking for my input.

After several such sessions that continued for months, it was time for my father to visit my brothers' prospective in-laws to inform them about the decision to delay the wedding dates. What transpired in those meetings remains unknown; however, we were told that of the three families, two had accepted the request on condition that there be no contact between the boys and girls. The third family immediately annulled the planned marriage.

This was not a total failure, except that Lemma Tessema doubted whether my father had revealed the true reason for the request to delay the marriage. We all knew that my father was not totally committed to our cause.

As the evening visits continued, I enjoyed the company of my brothers whom I had missed sorely during the last year. At the same time, a quiet guilt gnawed at my heart that I was surrounded by family members while my husband was cut off from the family he loved. More seriously, those evening meetings shortened the tender loving moments which we used for our mental health, love and intellectual growth. Many times, I risked my brothers' piercing disapproval when I crept so close to my husband, seeking body contact. In Siqualla, this was a sign of a woman with no decency.

Love continued to enrich our marriage. My husband was filled with love that he showed with an amazing restraint. Mine was love with an insatiable desire to see, hear and feel him. Liberated from the oppressive cultural taboos, I suddenly found the freedom to demand constant love, which my husband delivered with remarkable discipline. Every time I sought to delay that moment of oneness, he held me a bit tighter, offered one more kiss and revealed how much he enjoyed these moments.

"*Almaz,*" he said, "*You fill my heart with total happiness every time you embrace me. Yet, I am fully aware of your state of mind. Before I came into your life, you were a young woman admired for your beauty, wisdom and healing power. Today, you are a lonely bride, excluded from community. Your future is uncertain and your wish to become a mother is a distant dream.*

"*It pains me to say that I am waging this cultural war at your expense. But, today I give you my word of honour that you will become a mother; you will be the first female teacher in Siqualla and you will open your home to girls who will be inspired by your example and become the next teacher.*

"*Most of all, you will be known for our love: this genuine love that survived the test of time, strong love that stood against horrific odds, patient love that conquered the temptations of the flesh and generous love that is giving us the gift of enduring happiness.*"

Hearing my husband's feelings of love and guilt warmed my heart as I discreetly sought that dream moment of oneness, with no room between us for the wind to blow or the light to shine. As he did every time I desired him, he rubbed his forehead against mine and finished with a smile, teasing me,

"*I think my bride is in love with her husband. Isn't she?*"

I nodded yes and looked up to receive my daily gift of a kiss. This time, I deliberately pushed my head farther back so his lips could land on my mouth. I had had this joy only a few times. This time, I felt dizzy when his lips touched mine, but by the time I opened my eyes, his lips had moved to my forehead.

"*My love,*" he asked, "h*ow about a sip of water before I tell you the story of another historic figure from an ancient civilization?*"

He then told me about the amazing nation called India and its freedom fighter, Mahatma Gandhi, who used non-violence to free his country from a foreign rule. But, it seemed, Lemma Tessema had a different purpose in sharing this story for he brought up the unlikely subject of Gandhi's vow of *Brahmacharya,* the practice of self-control in thought, word and deed. As he proceeded to explain what a vow of restraint meant, I knew that there was a message for me in the story and asked myself,

"*Is he asking me to restrain my feelings? Has he been practising this vow of self-control without my knowledge?*"

I then realized that my husband, like me, did suffer from the same insatiable love with a maddening physical desire. In his case though, there was self-control inspired by Gandhi's vow of *Brahmacharya.* So I decided to let him know that I did get the subtle message of the story:

"*I regret that I have been exhibiting uncontrolled feelings because I lacked the benefit of your worldly knowledge. You seemed to have successfully kept yours away,*" I said.

Lemma Tessema jumped up, held my head with two hands and buried it in his chest.

"*No, my love, I want to see you desire me,*" he said, "*I am too much in love to take this vow. True, I have read Brahmacharya because I needed help to control my passion. But, I was not inspired by Gandhi's vow; you are my inspiration.*

"*My vow is to practise love that gives us equal joy, not one that hurts you. I confess that I am permanently burning with desire, but I will wait for you. We will enjoy true passion only when you are ready."*

Later that night, as I lay next to him, I saw a strange dream. In this dream, it was our wedding and we both looked like we did on the real day. There was the usual food and drink, music and dance with singers serenading us. We finally entered what looked like our private room where my husband forcefully carried out the *encounter*. When he forced himself inside me, blood streaming between my thighs, I screamed with terror, waking Lemma Tessema who instantly knew that I had a disturbing dream. When I refused to tell him the events in my dream, he seemed worried.

"*As long as it is not a wedding,*" he said and started to pray.

"*Our compassionate Lord, had it not been for the friendship of our fathers, there was hardly any chance for us to be united. But You brought us together because we are destined for a historic journey of love and courage.*

*"Lord, Almaz and I are feeling something that no word, song or poetry can describe. But, we both know that it is love. With this love, my wife has become my life and I am all Almaz has. I plead with You; help us live through this difficult period so we see the fruit of our love. Amen."*

Lemma Tessema was visibly frightened by what this dream could mean, but I knew that it was only a reflection of my most inner desire to know my husband, to receive his seed and carry his offspring. This feeling had been quietly growing inside me. Several times, I caught myself thinking that if I had braved the encounter on my wedding night, I would now be a respected mother-to-be or complaining that if Lemma Tessema had been a brave man, I would now be carrying a child.

I had carefully hidden these feelings until they finally decided to come out in a dream. But the groom in my dream could not be my husband. Lemma Tessema was a good man, nurturing me with boundless love, committed to giving me time to grow, and helping me become an informed woman with a choice.

# Chapter Eight

It was on this morning that I woke up with the headache that I had named Madam Thunder. When the holy water from St. Tekle-Haimanot Church failed, the elders agreed that a different treatment be tried. After poking and bleeding me, the medicine man ordered that I be taken to the big city for further treatment.

But this was the era when our country was run by the Satan, the Lucifer himself, known as the Black Stalin, who was murdering our people from one end of the country to the other. Our socialist leader had unleashed something called the red terror with a plan to turn villages into a map of ashes. So, Siqualla was completely cut off from the rest of the country with no access to the big city.

The morning I woke up with the headache, my husband already knew that I was unwell for he had been feeling my fever all night. But, what we ignored as a silly headache had lasted all day, giving us a serious concern. While I did not share his fear, I relented when Lemma Tessema insisted that I interrupt my studies for the evening so he could take care of me.

With my instructions, he prepared my herbal medicine which I snorted, sipped and pasted on my forehead. But my true medicine was my husband, holding me gently against his chest, his lips on my forehead and stroking my head with those alluring fingers. No ailment could fight back this medicine. I slept soundly all night.

In the morning, we were surprised when I woke up with the headache, this time worse. While it was not yet grave, I quietly rejoiced when my husband decided to stay home to look after me. Oh, how I craved for this day! But, my husband's only concern was to get rid of the headache as quickly as possible. As he kept asking about the nature and severity of the illness and comparing my response to the book he was consulting, I feared that he was going to waste my much desired day with trivial questioning.

Little did he know that his love was all I was after when I agreed that he spend the day at home, with me. So I complained.

"*My love, this is a simple headache; all I need is a brief respite.*"

As we say in Siqualla, "*The smart need only a hint; the fool a full detail.*"

My husband knew precisely what I meant by respite. He smiled, kissed me on the forehead and teased me, "*I think my bride is in love with her husband!*" He then promised to be with me all day on condition that I agreed to try his medicine. He then gave me a couple of pills that I swallowed, along with a huge dose of suspicion. I had little confidence in any medicine, other than my herbs.

Since our wedding day, my husband had been sowing seeds of love in my heart, one grain at a time. Today, a full tree was planted inside me when he carried me to the bed, my arms around his neck, my eyes locked against his, and chests pumping as if our hearts wanted to come out and meet. As he moved toward the bed, I wished that the room was bigger, or the bed was at the farthest corner or he stopped a bit longer, just a bit longer.

As if a clay pot, Lemma Tessema laid me down on the bed, slowly, gently, carefully. To my surprise, this rickety, squeaky piece of wood that threatened to fall apart every time we touched it, miraculously turned into a comfortable royal divan when he lay next to me, engulfed by a volcanic desire that looked beyond control. Here, we gazed at each other, our eyes communicating love in their own language.

As he pulled me toward him, I felt no fear, no resistance, only a strong passion, tempered by the Siqualla culture of shyness. My groom gently touched my lips.

"*My bride, do not be afraid,*" he said, "*I will never harm you. I no longer say this because I am convinced that you do trust me. I wish I could take your place today though, so you do not suffer this silly headache. I cannot bear to see you unhappy.*"

Lemma Tessema did not realize that the moment he lifted me from the ground, the headache was gone and when he laid me on the bed, I was transported to another life, outside this world. At this moment, words were unnecessary, so I simply took his arm, circled it around my waist and rested my head on the other arm. I then put my cheek against his, indirectly asking for more kisses. He obliged and began to kiss me, this time, longer, deeper, stronger.

Of all my happy days, there had never been a single moment when I tasted such a perfect happiness. As we continued to cuddle, kiss, merge, and burn, I could feel the steady growth of his thing, threatening to explode outside his trousers, as he looked embarrassed, fidgeting to keep it under control. It was on this day that we both experienced yet again the purest and sweetest of all affections that sent us both on a sound sleep for the entire morning.

When we woke up, it felt like a blink, but we had consumed an entire morning and part of the afternoon simply loving each other. Finally, it was time to get up, but my husband pulled me back, embracing me tight and asked me an important question.

"*Almaz,*" he said, "*you and I are united by genuine love and we share strong attraction for each other. Yet, we continue to keep our physical desire under control. How is this possible?*"

I agreed. Indeed, on this day, we both experienced the power of genuine love as husband and wife. We were transported where reason had no place. Yet, love prevailed and we conquered our physical desire because we knew that there would be no enjoyment if one of us was going to get hurt. We then concluded that the claim that love was the reason men forced women to engage in an *encounter* against their wish was baseless.

I then asked whether the saying, "*Dula*[12] *is a sign of love*" was justified.

"*Abuse and violence are not natural features of love,*" my husband responded, "*Rather they are borne out of inequality between women and men. Our love is strong because it is built on the principles of equality,*" he said and advised me, "*…to expose the error in the so-called logic that a violent man is a man in love, driven by jealousy.*"

To prepare me for my future role as a teacher, Lemma Tessema cautioned me to recognize those labels used to discredit brave women. Women with confidence and courage, women who spoke out and fought back, women

[12] beating

who questioned and challenged, women who discussed and debated were called loose, odd, cursed, crazy, scary, unwieldy, unattractive and undesirable. He then turned the subject back to our marriage, saying,

*"The more I love you, the clearer it has become for me that love is not blind. Love can see, feel and reason. This is the reason I also feel your pain because I am aware of your wish to become a mother.*

*"Almaz, you have already given me much happiness, but the day you call me Father of my Children would be the happiest in my life. This day cannot come soon enough for me. However, I have no desire to fulfill this wish if I am to cause you harm and pain."*

He assured me that our day was fast approaching and urged me to remain steadfast till our final victory. He concluded by saying,

*"Today, I wish to declare my true love and to dedicate my life to you, Almaz Tefera."*

With his gift for words, my husband had a way of entering my soul to stir my emotions and evoke tears which I started shedding as he continued to declare his love. As he consoled me, wiping my tears with bare hands, I took time to prepare my response, choosing my words carefully. It was important to declare my love in a way that he would remember for the rest of his life.

I told him that our love was built with sacrifices that changed our life forever. He had abandoned a comfortable urban life to bring knowledge to our people who no longer recognized him as one of them. Not long ago, our names were associated with beauty, love, and wisdom. Today, no one spoke of us. We started off our married life as a prosperous couple only to end up with no land, no home and no property. All this was the sacrifice paid by my husband because of his love for his wife and his determination to protect my wellbeing and happiness.

I complimented my husband that in the two years of our marriage, he transformed me from a woman with fear to a woman in love. I confessed that I no longer worried every night whether it was going to be the night of my virginity test. Rather, I longed for his soothing warmth, gentle caress and kind words. Hearing his voice no longer evoked fear in me, instead I felt like a child whose mother had just come back from the market with a sugar cane.

*"Thanks to your perseverance with my education, I am convinced that I can do more than merely breeding babies. You have shown me my value as a human being, a woman, a mother and a citizen. I can now see my potential outside the kitchen; I am on my way to become the first female teacher in Siqualla and mother of two,"* I added.

Speaking about our love, I said that it was a gift that sustained me when I despaired, consoled me when I grieved and filled my heart with hope in my sadness. I told him that I had no desire for any precious pendant as I would be wearing his love my entire life. I assured him that I would support him for as long as I lived since I knew he was quietly grieving the loss of his much loved family.

*"To fill the vacuum created in your life, I promise to strive to be like a sister, a mother and a friend to you. I am yours for ever, my love,"* I concluded.

I could detect the enormous effect this had on my husband, as he looked away to hide the urge for weeping. I quickly left the bed and headed toward the kitchen, while he remained frozen with feelings.

As hope faded, we faced the grim fact that there might not be a cure for me. With this news, grief covered the entire village like the veil of a mourning mother. Although in Siqualla we had lost leaders, warriors, elders and men and women, none had caused the kind of grief felt over me. It looked like my village had finally a complete change of heart about me.

Indeed, the village was drowning in a collective fear that it was to become the second Golgotha where love was to be crucified. Filled with guilt, the villagers started to engage in an exchange of criticism against their creator, their leaders and each other.

"*God does not seem to have eyes for others. Why Almaz again?*" they complained.

"*Let's not blame our Lord,*" others responded, "*He is not here to defend Himself. We know who is responsible for this tragedy. It is our own unkindness.*"

"*It is our elders who pushed her to this, questioning her ability to bear children.*"

"*We all know the true culprit, don't we? The so-called schooled man!*"

Having seen the mental state of the community, the elders decided to intervene.

"*If you find a snake in your cottage,*" they said, "*do you first kill it or do you go around looking for the opening it came through? We have a bride about to die and you are busy apportioning blame.*

"*Don't we say it takes a village to raise a child? If we had failed Almaz, there is then a culprit in each one of us. It is now time to think of solutions and not to find culprits*"

But, the villagers were too burdened with grief and guilt to think right. So, they were asked to go back home and pray while the elders met privately. Our elders had enormous influence over the villagers who always listened to their advice, respected their orders and trusted their judgment. In return, the elders who often made life-and-death decisions discharged their duties with the heavy weight of responsibility.

Often, they isolated themselves from the outside world to seek God's guidance and to sharpen their insight into taking the right course of action. This time, the assembly spent the entire night, seeking input from villagers, collecting community intelligence about safe routes to the big city, praying for God's guidance and weighing the potential risks of the various options to be considered.

Finally, the elders admitted that they felt inadequate for the job at hand because failure could mean the death of a bride who had no one to carry her name, except her good name as a beautiful girl, a wise woman and a committed wife.

Before dawn, the elders' assembly assigned a representative to present the full report of their decision to the villagers, going back to the beginning of how it all started when I was let down by the same community that raised me. He reminded the villagers that, once praised as a symbol of love and beauty, it took a single misfortune for the entire village to turn against us when it was known that we produced a false result of the virginity test, leading to a malicious suspicion that we were in fact trying to hide my infertility.

The speaker then presented my husband's version of the story:

*"Tonight, the elders were told by Lemma Tessema that what happened on the wedding night had nothing to do with Almaz. It was not her wish nor had she planned it. It was her husband's. Her husband had assured the assembly that the couple was not trying to hide Almaz's infertility.*

*"He told us that his objective was to give his wife time to grow both mentally and physically so she was well prepared for her new life as a mother. Lemma Tessema is still committed to this decision, even if it meant going against Siqualla's values.*

*"Having heard this background, the elders were remorseful of the community's action against the couple. After long and sober consultations, the assembly has agreed unanimously that, since there is no access to the capital city, Almaz should be taken to a neighbouring country where she can receive treatment for this mysterious disease and brought back to her marriage, her community and her village.*

*"As you all know, going to the neighbouring country, we will have to follow the route familiar to the political refugees whom we often shelter here as they flee the demonic army. While long and difficult, this route has so far remained unknown, so we should be safe, as long as this information stays here.*

*"We need to be well prepared for this fateful journey as we will be carrying a near-dead woman through a long barren land, filled with wildlife, bandits, and often visited by nature's fury. Almaz might not make it, but we would rather fail trying than fail to try.*

*"At the request of her husband, the assembly has also made a solemn vow that, if our Lord spares Almaz's life, we will commit to stopping the practice of female circumcision, the virginity test and to raising the marriage age throughout the village.*

*"This is our Kassa to God for having destroyed a beautiful marriage, for sentencing a wonderful couple to dislocation, homelessness and isolation and for subjecting Almaz to inhuman treatment, simply because she was suspected to be infertile, as if children were hand made by women.*

*"We recognize that the proposed measures are drastic and revolutionary, but, they are not beyond our will or capacity. So, they will be implemented on voluntary basis in every home, by every family, throughout the village, no exception.*

*"In the name of St. Tekle-Haimanot, the elders request every father, grandfather, son, brother and husband to accept the vow as if it were one of the 10 Commandments.*

*"Siqualla is now ready for change. On this matter; we shall no longer make excuses, offer cooperation, remain indifferent, look away, be quiet or pretend ignorance,"* he concluded.

The villagers were then told that an advance group had already left to convey a message to every hamlet along the way to expect a sick refugee who needed to be looked after. The same group was also asked to secure hiding places and prepare burial sites for my final resting place, should this be my fate.

With this news, Siqualla, the land of brave men and women who survived death, loss and grief, crumbled under the grim prospect of my passing. As villagers headed back to their homes, they mused over the unexpectedness of things,

*"Why take* a d*ying woman to a foreign land? Shouldn't she stay put in her homeland where she is entitled to a final resting place?"*

*"Why bury her elsewhere? Since when do* we *abandon one of our own, dead or alive?"*

*"Why bring up a simple matter like the virginity test now? Of course, this is the work of you know who! Lemma Tessema finally got what he has been plotting all along."*

Siqualla had always a way of coming together in spite of bitter divisions. This time too, the village came out united from East to West; North to South. Every family assigned one or two male volunteers to accompany me, loaned a donkey or a horse for transportation and offered food for the travelling company. Women were asked to stay behind and continue their care giving duties to the families who sent volunteers.

In the morning, unified as one force, the travelling mass assembled, stretching for as far as the eyes could see. In this vast gathering of volunteers, there were the entire family of my in-laws, my own family of five men, uncles and nephews, as well as men as old as eighty and boys as young as ten. The St. Tekle-Haimanot Church volunteered a group of clergymen to join the travelling group, apparently with a secret plan to officiate my funeral.

Looking at the size of the travelling mass, the leaders decided to cut the group into a manageable size by disallowing elderly men, boys and persons with disability to join the trip. This displeased far too many people, but the orders were respected nonetheless.

When we started the journey, the stretcher was carried by four men, led by my weeping husband. Dozens followed to take their turns. Dressed in my late mother's wedding gown, my face covered with a veil, and a white cloth draped over me, I looked like I was on my way to the cemetery. When they carried me out of the cottage, I heard what I thought was a huge thunder, but no, this was the collective cry of the villagers, grieving my imminent death. Indeed, this was my funeral, but I was yet to die.

Known for their haunting wailing that churns the stomach, shedding tears that run down their neck, Siquallans then lamented,

"*It is not yet your turn, Almaz, you still have much to live, much to see, much to enjoy.*

"*We grieve for you, Lemma, how are you to survive this tragedy?*

"*Oh, you unkind death, how dare you take the best and brightest among us!*

"*Lord, please do not make Siqualla the graveyard of a beautiful love.*"

# Chapter Nine

As we travelled across the village, the entire population came out in prayer, and grief. Carrying the picture of St. Tekle-Haimanot, people stood outside their cottages or lined up the roads, bidding me farewell as if this was the final adieu. Hearing the immense collective grief, I realized that I had indeed been a much loved daughter of this village. Or, as we say in Siqualla, "*Do we all become good only in death*?"

After travelling the whole morning, those who were not part of the travelling team were asked to return and inform the community about our safe arrival in the neighbouring village where an earlier delegation had already delivered the news of my expected arrival. Here, the leaders were surprised by the reception given me, with countless people ready to join the march, dozens of homes open to welcome me and bountiful of food and drink prepared to feed the travelling army. Having spent more time than planned, it was decided to spend the night in this welcoming village and regroup the next day to proceed to the next destination.

For days, we travelled safely; only the sun remained unkind, forcing us to change our journey from day to night. But, with torches that turned the night into midday, we could easily avoid dangerous spots and creatures. All in all, the plan was well executed as every hamlet welcomed us with resting places, fresh food and eager volunteers.

A few times, we came across political refugees who shared valuable information about the safest and fastest routes. Some volunteered to make the trip with us, even if this was to delay their own journey.

With the steady deterioration of my condition, my husband had become a major hurdle as he kept insisting that we take long breaks even when not warranted. While the volunteers took turns to rest, he remained steady on my side, carrying the stretcher until he could no longer walk. When finally relieved, he would come to my side, hold my hand and walk; then move to the other side, hold the other hand, constantly checking,

"*Can you feel me, my love?*"

"*We are almost there, my bride, be brave.*"

"*I am here, my darling, I will never leave you.*"

From his questions, I knew that my husband was both physically exhausted and mentally traumatized and I wept internally with guilt that I was, once more, responsible for this suffering. This man who once unleashed unimaginable terror in me was now a victim of my own misfortunes. As I always do when I feel love, I so wanted to be with him again, that moment of oneness, held tightly, my head on his chest and his lips on my forehead. But, it was not to be. By all accounts, I was as good as dead and he was almost a widower.

On Day Five, having walked all night, the leaders decided to give the volunteers time to rest, heal, and recover their energy. We were all looking forward to putting this day behind us so to cross the riskiest part of the journey, infested with vengeful mosquitoes and snakes, cursed with a hostile environment and inhabited by a population with a reputation for inhospitality. For political refugees, this last leg of flight represented the final deadly frontier before they crossed to the neighbouring country. For me, it was to be the dawn of my second chance. But God had ordained it for a different fate.

The next day, we were about to resume the arduous journey when I heard the little internal voice that always spoke to me when danger loomed in the horizon. In a message I could not decipher, this little voice spoke about something ominous and I feared that this was to be my final resting place. So, I tried to come up with excuses to delay our departure, leaving the leaders puzzled as to what was the reason behind this.

Throughout the journey, I had been a model patient, complimented for my cooperation. The leaders had told my husband several times that while they were impressed by my resilience; they were disappointed by how weak he had proven to be in facing our fate. But, on this day, my attempt to delay the most critical part of the journey had the leaders worried.

Having failed to delay the departure, I finally asked for a private meeting with my husband to try to convince him to postpone the trip. Of course, with so many leaders, he was not in a position to handle such an important matter independently. So, he presented the request for the leaders' consideration but their response was negative.

"*We are too near our long-sought objective to delay. After all, only time is standing between Almaz's life and her death. Our plan is to take her back home; not to bury her here.*"

No sooner had we resumed the journey when we landed on a scorched piece of earth that was searing not only from the sun above but also from the ground below. Many before us had apparently perished here, appropriately called the Bereavement Field. As we continued our march, I could hear the volunteers cry in pain, as their sandals melted and their feet were covered with oozing blisters.

With no village in sight, the leaders soon started to ration water, and prepare rescue plans in the event that a large number of volunteers succumbed. While this leg of the journey was the grimmest, knowing that we were only a day away from our final destination gave the group a much needed boost to persevere.

As we pressed on, the force dwindled considerably as many fell ill due to injury, disease or sheer fright. Regardless, good will was still in abundance as those who braved the condition came forward with valour to replace the fallen heroes. Some who used up their stamina were exempted from the remaining journey. Among those asked to return were my father and father-in-law, along with a couple of elderly priests, and a few who sustained serious injuries. All brothers, by blood, marriage, or neighbourhood, remained firm, declaring their decision,

"*We will return only when Almaz is ready to walk back with us.*"

After a rough, thorny and perilous trek, I was left alone under a lone tree for a rather long time while the volunteers kept busy nursing the sick and injured. Having spent enough time with these volunteers, I could tell that, this time, there was a sudden change in the group's demeanour. At some point, it felt as if the volunteers had abandoned me and I was left all alone in this forbidding piece of hell.

As I paid closer attention, I noticed that the litany of complaints about blisters and bites; the screams of volunteers attacked by vicious mosquitoes; the call for help as thorns were pulled out, along with pieces of flesh; and the plea for a drop of water were gone. The group's familiar tone of optimism, the sound of determination, and songs of bravery were also silenced. Instead, I sensed a frightening mood of disbelief and panic. But, I could not make out what was happening.

Gradually, the conversation among the volunteers turned into a whispered, "hush, hush", as if they were keeping a secret from me. As I strained my hearing, I was able to detect sounds of muffled cry, quiet argument and a general feeling of terror. This was followed by what felt like chaos as if the group had suffered a loss. There were several attempts to distract my attention away from this chaos, but I kept asking for my husband, until they finally responded.

"*Your husband is down with malaria and he had forgotten to carry both your herbal medicine and his malaria pills.*"

Almost blind, nearly deaf and about to die, I could not understand what this information entailed and kept calling, "*Lemma Tessema*". One of the priests touched my forehead with a cross, said a quick prayer and explained that my husband had fallen ill with the recurrent malaria and was too sick to take care of me. What I did next shocked the entire living being. I jumped out of my stretcher, crawled on the ground and howled like a wounded beast before I passed out.

My husband knew immediately that I was told about his illness and insisted on coming to my stretcher. Here, we were laid next to each other, two corpses, only love alive in our hearts. When I finally regained sense, we were both burning as if we were put on a pyre. My skin was melting like wax from the fever that was quietly consuming my husband with little mercy. But, I was determined to burn with him.

Desperate to save us from the invisible inferno, the volunteers kept dowsing us with their share of water until they used up the last drop.

When I realized that he was barely conscious, I kissed his hand which I laboured to bring up to my lips and said, "*Father of my children, I am here with you.*" Lemma Tessema responded. By love's mysterious power, he summoned his last bit of energy to stretch his arm which he slid under, and pulled me towards him with such force that we achieved the oneness of love.

I tugged my face inside his neck and we continued to burn like two bright torches. We defied the dark reality of the Bereavement Field, and our love triumphed over the cruel malaria. As hope and desperation hovered over us, we fought death with courage as it threatened to murder our precious love.

In the morning, we saw the last dawn of our beautiful life. Our eyes met briefly and we managed to say an incoherent "*I love you*" just before my husband took his last breath. It was only then that I remembered my wedding dream; an omen of death. Yes, death had been eyeing my husband for some time.

The visionary who brought an ancient village out of darkness, the brave man who stood up for women, the passionate groom who knew the meaning of love died in a desolate land. With the audacity that dared the permanence of death, my husband left this earth filled with love. As he made his last exit, I could see the splendour that captivated me on our wedding night. He showed no fear or regret, only the same passion that shone through his eyes the day he carried me to the bed.

Later that day, I was carried on a stretcher to his funeral and he was laid to rest in the same grave I was meant to occupy. Aged sixteen, I became a widow. I buried a twenty-three old groom who died on my behalf. Telling you this, I should be weeping blood, but I had since been filled with emptiness and my eyes had run out of tears. Dry like desert sand, my heart was drained of all human feelings.

As we say in Siqualla, "*God never gives a load we cannot carry*." Miraculously, I came out alive of the Bereavement Field and on the sixth day of the journey, we arrived in the borders of the neighbouring country. I was immediately taken to a refugee camp where I was interviewed to determine whether I was a legitimate refugee. Distinctly different from the UN definition of persecution based on race, religion or political affiliation, my story did not match the UN category of refugees. I was registered as "a victim of harmful cultural practices."

A proud Ethiopian, I, Almaz Tefera, the much desired daughter, the precious love of Lemma Tessema, the stunning beauty of Siqualla and the miraculous healer had joined the refugee family, identified by a number on a piece of card. I was now among those whose only hope was to be alive.

A visionary endowed with courage, love and splendour had died for me, yet in a single day, I became one of the most dispensable human beings in the world. When I was told that, as a refugee, I could be raped, mutilated, murdered, burnt alive or left to drown, I consoled myself that at least Lemma Tessema was not alive to witness this inhumanity.

The next day, I was taken to the *Médecins sans Frontières* clinic where I had undergone extensive medical tests that revealed the cause of the so-called Madam Thunder: a vicious brain tumour. Promptly, a team of medical professionals, led by Canadian surgeon Rob Caldwell, was put together to operate on me. To the surprise of the entire population in the refugee camp, I was given such an unprecedented priority that I felt as if the Queen of Sheba herself had gone to exile from her Kingdom.

As the nurses prepared me for the surgery, I could tell from their blank faces that this was a hopeless case, the beginning of my end. But little did they know that I was never meant to die! And true, after three-months in intensive care, I came out of coma with my sight and hearing restored. A few days later, the doctors still jubilant with their partial success, I uttered my first words, "*Lemma Tessema.*" This moved the entire medical team to tears since news about my loss was already known in and beyond the refugee camp.

Recovery was long, lonely and difficult. After a long stay, members of my travelling army had left in twos and threes in order to catch up with the farming season. Ordered to leave the country, my brothers were convinced that I had run out of luck and was about to lose the battle. As far as Siqualla was concerned, the news was that Lemma Tessema was lost in a forsaken land while Almaz Tefera was left in a foreign land, waiting for a final resting place.

It was now more than a year since my surgery, a period filled with emotions of denial, anger, grief and anxiety. There was not much else left for my brain to suffer when, at long last, I started bouncing back, showing signs of life. A faint hope had finally emerged that I was slowly becoming a full human being with sight, hearing, speech and finally mobility. Only my heart refused to heal, understandably.

It was about this time that a young man arrived from my village to deliver a message from my family. According to this messenger, a historic transformation had taken place in Siqualla, following a massive campaign to end the harmful cultural practices that kept our society backward for far too long. This campaign, named after my late husband, was in response to the promise the elders made when they decided to send me to the neighbouring country for treatment.

Thanks to the knowledge given them by my late husband, my brothers took charge of the uprising, educating the community about the negative social norms, harmful cultural practices, preferential family treatments and attitudes towards women and girls. The young volunteers who travelled with me also played a key role, mobilizing the community which was divided into two camps, one supporting and the other opposing the change.

As the two camps embarked on a bitter fight, the government intervened, singling out the volunteers, accusing them of counter-revolutionary activities. It was charged that the cultural revolt was, in fact, incited by the late Lemma Tessema, the rebellious man who instigated an exodus of an entire village with the pretext of seeking a cure for his infertile wife. This unfair charge triggered a protest that engulfed the entire community.

In what ensued, countless peasants were imprisoned. To a village that had never known a prison in its entire history; this was enough to ignite an angry peasant uprising with no return. The government had no choice but to fight this war out, but Siqualla was no ordinary enemy. This was when the village lived up to the old saying,

*"Siqualla is soft enough to bend for friendship but firm enough to break in hostility."*

Indeed, the village stood firm until the government had to concede defeat; and quietly released every prisoner, urging the population to resume normal life.

Again, as it had done throughout its history, Siqualla showed its ability to put divisions aside in favour of unity. It was at the end of this conflict that the community came together to make history by declaring Siqualla free of the harmful cultural practices: early, child and forced marriage, FGM, virginity test and the ill-treatment of women who were or suspected to be infertile.

With much regret, the messenger informed me that this historic triumph had had an unfortunate huge blotch because the government had declared me "*persona non grata*" for leaving the country in protest of the revolution. Because of the support given it by some disgruntled elements, the government was also emboldened into issuing a warning that any family or individual who sheltered, supported or hid me was liable to the same charges under the *Protection of the Socialist Revolution Act.*

This frightened my family into sending a secret message.

"*If you are still alive,*" read the letter, "*We thank our beloved St. Tekle-Haimanot for having spared you the hands of the government. Had your husband lived, he would have faced the bullets of the revolutionary army. You would have spent your life in prison, a place we have all survived with permanent scars.*

"*But the Lord is still on our side for we have prevailed. Walk with your heart full of pride. Your husband did not die in vain. We have shed precious blood to achieve what he stood for. His name will remain engraved in our history and we shall honour his legacy as the man who transformed Siqualla.*

"*While we have entered a new era of equality, our victory is hollow for we shall never see you again. We will never heal from the pain of this loss, but we will find solace in knowing that our daughters will now grow up in an equal society, with opportunities to gain knowledge, build capacity, and realize their potential.*

*"May St. Tekle-Haimanot be with you."*

# Chapter Ten

My heart which was emptied of all human feelings following the death of my husband suddenly felt joy and I was filled with pride to hear about his legacy. Lemma Tessema had refused to know me, so I could mature, become a woman, enjoy motherhood, and achieve self-sufficiency. But he did not live to see the fruits of his sacrifice. Worse, I would never set foot in that land to witness the positive changes that came about for women as a result of his vision.

No sooner had I felt a glimmer of joy when my heart was again filled with the deepest sense of sadness, realizing that I had now lost my motherland as well. If there was any doubt in my mind about my new identity, here was a proof that I had indeed become a refugee.

Suddenly, I felt a strong need for a country where I would be called Ethiopian, the daughter of Tefera, the wife of Lemma Tessema, the child of Siqualla. I wanted to be known, to be accepted, to belong, to be trusted and never to be questioned. I so wanted to be in Ethiopia, my motherland with its female circumcision, virginity test and fistula. Yes, with all its vices, I missed Siqualla. As we say in my village,

*"The bond between a nation and its citizen always remains where the umbilical cord is buried."*

Months later, Dr. Rob Caldwell entered my room with a young woman he introduced as a translator. With her assistance, he inquired about my health and, for the first time, gave me the full story of my surgery and recovery with details as to how the team fought to save my life. He told me that I was named "The Miracle Jewel" because I kept coming back every time they thought they had lost me. I had apparently had several setbacks, including serious infections that required them to take risky decisions.

This Canadian surgeon who had taken me under his wing throughout this ordeal was now embarking on another life-saving mission.

"*I think that the one-legged saint of your village is still protecting you,*" he teased me. "*Today, I can say with confidence that you have recovered fully. The time has now come to prepare you for life outside the Médecins sans Frontières clinic. What do you wish to do, Almaz?*"

I told the good doctor that if it was determined that I was well enough, I was ready to go look for my husband's grave and take his remains for a proper burial in our village. My only wish in life was to honour Lemma Tessema not only for his accomplishments but also for dying for love. I shared with the doctor my plan to open a school in my husband's name and spend the rest of my life, educating about a fair and equal society, free from the barriers that prevented women and girls from realizing their potential.

I continued, "*My husband was a truly strong man who died for the love of his wife. He was against violence perpetrated against women in the name of love, jealousy, family honour, personal reputation or social respectability. I will dedicate my life to ensuring that the principles he stood for were held high in every society.*"

Dr. Caldwell was impressed and genuinely happy that I was indeed well enough to think this far. But he reminded me that I had no longer a country to go back to and urged me to be strong enough in accepting my new fate not only as a widow, but also as a stateless refugee. It was during this conversation that the name Canada was mentioned for the first time by the doctor who suggested that I appeal to this country for asylum.

In making the suggestion, Dr. Caldwell said this about the country,

"Canada *is where slaves from America escaped to in search of freedom. Among those slaves was a woman called Harriet Tubman who made 19 trips to bring her people out of slavery in America to freedom in Canada. You will be the modern Harriet Tubman, minus the Underground Railroad. Here, you can promote your husband's vision because equality between women and men is still elusive throughout the world.*"

My application for refugee sponsorship was submitted within days, but it took three years for my case to be processed and approved. During the waiting period, I attended class for refugees, volunteered in hospitals and clinics, read books and wrote poems, while educating myself about the place of women in different societies.

Now my eyes focused beyond Siqualla, I was saddened to see that this world was not yet good for women. In fact, Siqualla stood out as the better. This reminded me of a popular advice told by our elders, "*Do not leave home for you might end up in worse places.*"

Now that I was aware of the past treatment and current status of women and girls, I wished my husband was alive because there was still much to do to make this world right.

At times, I pondered whether Lemma Tessema was aware that, across our planet, there were societies where:

*Women were used as sex supplies in something called pornography,*

*Women were disfigured by acid thrown by men they jilted,*

*Women were killed in the name of family honour,*

*Girls were sold and bought for sex trade,*

*Migrant women workers were exploited, raped and murdered,*

*Refugee women were forced to make sexual favours by officials,*

*Women simply went missing or were found murdered.*

While broadening my knowledge about women in societies, I kept busy, keeping afloat in this life of uncertainty, filled with the daily indignities of identity checks, hostility, and threats. The worst of it all was the constant reminder that I was the most unwanted and easily dispensable refugee. My patience tested to the limit, I felt tired of it all, the transient life with no change. Throughout, I remained in denial about my fate, often asking myself:

"*What happened? Why am I here and not in Siqualla?*

*"Where is my life, the one with a loving husband and two children?*

*"How do I face the future without Lemma Tessema?*"

Eager to open a new chapter, I started to imagine my life in Canada. It was at this time that a poem written for Canada was read out in our refugee class, even though most of us had little knowledge about the language. Much longer in its entirety, the poem was explained to the class stanza by stanza to show its relevance to refugees.

I'm on my way to Canada,  
That old and dreary land,  
The dire effects of slavery,  
I can no longer stand.

My bone is vexed within me,  
To think that I am slave,  
And now resolved to strike the blow,  
For freedom or the grave.

Oh, Righteous Father, wilt thou pity me,  
And aid me to Canada, where coloured men are free.

I was so touched by the message that I decided to memorize the poem, reciting it every night as part of my daily prayer, replacing the last lines for:

"*Oh, St. Tekle-Haimanot, aid me to Canada where refugees can be free.*"

Finally, my prayers were answered; my application was accepted; the immigration papers had arrived. The time had now come to assume yet another identity as an immigrant, to join a new society across the ocean and to acquire a fresh set of survival skills.

In preparing myself for the future, I looked back at my life as a refugee to measure the extent of the hardships I survived in the last four years. To my astonishment, I felt nothing but a great sense of gratitude to this neighbouring country, called the Sudan.

Yes, the Sudan had sheltered me for four years and its people shared their space with complete strangers like me. I quietly admitted to myself that in this great country I had had several happy occasions like the Ramadan, Eid-al-Fitr and Eid-al-Adha which I celebrated with followers of the Prophet Mohamed, who showered me with gifts of dates, henna and perfume. Here, I was taught a new language which I spoke fluently by the time I left. Feeling indebted to this land of generous people, I wept for my second homeland which I was about to leave.

The year was 1990. I boarded a plane bound to Canada as a 20-year old mature woman, a widow of a remarkable man who empowered me with love, courage and hope. I was no longer the little girl of Siqualla, the child bride suspected of infertility, the young victim of harmful cultural practices, and the vile wife who produced fake virginity test result.

I had been transformed; a brave woman who survived loss, the refugee who refused to be dispensed. I was an informed, confident woman, with infinite potential for self-sufficiency, ready to contribute to society and determined to pull others as I climb up.

At long last, I entered the old dreary land of freedom. On arrival, I shed tears of joy and my heart smiled with hope. As I was exiting the airport, I saw a huge screen with three words flickering consistently. I stopped to read each letter slowly, "W e l c o m e  T o  C a n a d a ." Such a nice phrase, I said, wiping tears, as I responded quietly,

*"Thank you, Canada. I promise to help you build a society where men stand up for women, boys speak out for girls and husbands give their life for the love of their wives. I mean men like my husband, the late Lemma Tessema."*